SMALL CHANGE

A Richard Jackson Book

SMALL CHANGE

MARC TALBERT

DORLING KINDERSLEY PUBLISHING, INC.

A Richard Jackson Book

Dorling Kindersley Publishing, Inc.
95 Madison Avenue
New York, New York 10016

Visit us on the World Wide Web at http://www.dk.com

Dorling Kindersley books are available at special discounts for bulk
purchases for sales promotions or premiums. Special editions, including
personalized covers, excerpts of existing guides, and corporate imprints
can be created in large quantities for specific needs. For more information,
contact Special Markets Dept., Dorling Kindersley Publishing, Inc.,
95 Madison Ave., New York, NY 10016; fax: (800) 600-9098.

Library of Congress Cataloging-in-Publication Data
Talbert, Marc. [date]
Small change / by Marc Talbert.—1st ed.
p.   cm.
Summary: When a band of armed men creates
a disruption in the small Mexican town where Tom and his
younger sister Philippa are vacationing with their parents,
they flee into the hills with their new friend Ignacio.
ISBN: 0-7894-2531-9
[1. Mexico—Fiction.] I. Title.
PZ7.T14145 Sm 2000   [Fic]—dc21   99-046462

Book design by Annemarie Redmond.
The text of this book is set in 13 point Aldus.

Printed and bound in U.S.A.

First Edition, 2000
2 4 6 8 10 9 7 5 3 1

For

Sonja, Greg, and Chloe Bohanon
and with special thanks to an extraordinary editor,
Dick Jackson

CHAPTER ONE

Sunday. On a Mexican beach. Puffs of warm air lifting the bleached hair on his forearm. A startling blue sky. Sunlight slipping off his oiled skin.

Yet miserable.

Tom would rather have been anyplace else but here—anyplace where people at least spoke English. He strained to understand the gibberish around him, and, when he couldn't, it all made him feel stupid.

And trapped. With nobody to talk to, his thoughts bumped rudely into each other as they tried escaping what seemed like dryer lint clogging his head. As for escaping this beach, the dumpy hotel didn't even have a swimming pool. As for escaping the hotel, Tom didn't know how to get anywhere, anyhow—even if there were someplace better nearby, which he doubted.

Bore, boring, bored. How did Mexicans say *bored*

in Spanish? Being here was like reading the menu of a fast-food Mexican restaurant: El Boring Mucho. El Boring Grande. El Boring Supremo with Guacamole.

There wasn't anything to do except eat, sleep, splash in the water, and fry in the sun. It was a miracle that all the lumps of vacationing lard lying around the beach didn't smell like bacon cooking.

Nobody back home would believe him, but Tom missed the cold and snow and ice and dark of Minnesota. He would much rather have been there than here—even ice fishing with his uncle Tucker. He thought about the hut covered with tar paper in the middle of Wasp Lake, guarding its hole like an Arctic outhouse. Even with ice cubes for toes he'd rather be there.

He glanced at his younger sister, Philippa, who was building a sand castle a few feet away with Gordon, an eight-year-old boy from Seattle she'd met when they'd arrived two days ago. The two of them were talking and scolding and laughing and arguing with each other as easily as if they'd been best friends forever. Why was it that she always made friends so easily, and he couldn't?

His eyes darted to the cluster of nuts poised to drop from the shaggy top of a coconut tree. What were the nuts waiting for? His gaze plummeted, landing on the sand castle . . . KA-BOOM! The towers and walls were cracked and falling apart, looking as if they'd been bombed already.

Tom sighed and let his eyes drift along the curved white crescent of the beach. His parents had taken off on a walk an hour ago, hand in hand, and Tom couldn't make them out from the other fly specks at the sand's far end.

Except that he had to watch Philippa, he was glad they were gone. For the past two days, he hadn't liked being seen with them in public. They'd come here—to this beach, to this hotel—on their honeymoon fifteen years ago, and they'd been acting lovesick since they all got off the plane in Felicidad.

They were constantly touching each other in ways that parents shouldn't—holding hands, rubbing cheeks together, running fingers through each other's hair. It was disgusting.

They were so infected with this love bug that last evening, on the hotel's terrace, they'd bought beers and forgotten to drink them as they gazed at each other. They'd looked like a video on pause. Not even Tom and Philippa's bickering had distracted them. By the time they remembered the beer—and Tom and Philippa—the sun had gone down and the sweat had dried from the bottles.

He tensed, noticing a small Mexican boy walking toward him. The boy was wearing a Cowboys T-shirt and tiny gym shorts with frayed purple piping around the edges. His oily hair was stringy with dirt and he had a ragged scar over one eyebrow. He was so skinny that his elbow joints were larger than his biceps.

Tom hoped the kid would walk past him. Fat chance. Already five other kids had stopped this morning, hawking jewelry or Chiclets or little carvings.

Before Tom could say anything, the boy smiled. He was missing a lot of teeth, even for a kid that age. And before Tom knew it, the boy plunked a carved stone dolphin into his hand.

"Hey!" Tom sputtered, thrusting it back toward the boy.

The boy nodded, which made his smile bounce.

"Four *dólares,* amigo," he said, lisping.

Tom steadied himself in his chair. "No!" He shook the dolphin at the boy.

The boy took a step back. His smile grew, as if he thought this was a game. "Three *dólares,*" he said.

"Geez!" Rudeness was the only thing these kids seemed to understand. He turned the dolphin over in his hand and saw a small oval sticker on the bottom that said: Made in China.

He squinted up at the boy. "You made this?" The boy nodded happily. "And it was blessed by Mother Teresa?" Tom continued.

Once more the boy nodded happily. His smile barely flinched when Tom dropped the dolphin into the sand. The boy picked it up and then began whistling.

Whistling! This kid probably had nothing except the clothes he wore. No shoes. No teeth. No nothing. He was selling junk from China. He probably hadn't eaten well in days. He'd just been made fun of. *And he was whistling!*

Philippa was scolding Gordon about collapsing a wall as the boy walked up to them. He stopped whistling and stood watching, looking as if he wanted to join in. Philippa and Gordon ignored him. As cautiously as if he were petting a strange dog, the boy touched Philippa's hair. Mexicans were always doing that, as if blond hair were more special than black. Without looking, Philippa slapped the hand away as if it were a bug.

Not seeming the least bit bothered, the boy straightened his shoulders and began to whistle again. Tom watched in amazement as he walked right through a soccer game that some older bare-chested Mexican boys in jeans were playing, with the water as one boundary and a heel-dug trench the other.

Tom winced each time they kicked the ball hard with their bare feet. This was supposed to be fun? They threw themselves at the ball, at the sand, at each other. When the ball flew into the water, several of them dove to retrieve it. After wrestling and splashing, they'd slog out of the water looking so re-freshed that Tom decided they kicked the ball into the water on purpose most of the time. They might as well have been playing tackle football without helmets.

His stomach growled even though he'd finished off a bag of potato chips not too long ago. It had to be after noon, but he didn't know for sure—wearing a watch would have ruined his tan. He was tempted to drag Philippa to the beach restaurant next to the hotel and order some food that hadn't come from the ocean. But he was feeling sun drunk, with as much energy as a stranded fish roasting slowly on the beach.

Tom stared at the ocean. Shards of light, sharp as needles, shot through his otherwise armorlike, wrap-around sunglasses, making his eyes water. He longed to turn off the sound of the waves but they only seemed to grow louder when he tried to ignore

them. He watched the waves. Their tongues popped
out, hissing, when they tripped, falling over. They'd
sprawl and then retreat, leaving spent foam drib-
bling down the skinlike sand. Then they'd take a
breath and make another assault on the land, only to
trip again.

Tom looked from the waves to the beach, raked
clean now, except for the gaps between hotels and
restaurants where piles of garbage collected. In the
blazing sunlight, the beach was very different from
what he'd seen before breakfast the past two morn-
ings. Then, the whole expanse had been littered with
dead and rotting things. What looked from a distance like huge droppings from a sick horse turned
out to be piles of seaweed. And there were hundreds
of fish and squid, broken crabs and still-pulsing
blobs of jellyfish looking like gobs of snotty spit
come to life. Some of the carcasses had been chewed
on—probably by a couple of dogs he'd seen roaming
the beaches—but never the spiky puff fish, which,
with their bloated bodies and pouty mouths frozen
into balloon-tip kisses, were the most interesting to
look at. They reminded Tom of some of the weird
kids back home. All these fish needed were lip rings.

The thought of this almost made him smile, but
he caught himself in time. Thank God for his sun-

glasses. They were as sleek and tapered as the cockpit windows of a jet. Nobody could see what he was looking at or guess what he was feeling. He could be a spy, taking photos of all the people on this beach each time he blinked his shutterlike camera eyes.

He'd been spying a lot, even though the targets hadn't been very good—except for the occasional soldier walking by. He'd expected the beach to be swarming with girls ready to burst out of tiny swimsuits. Instead, only a couple of girls had been worth looking at, and nobody was as cute as Laura, his almost-girlfriend back home.

Tom couldn't help feeling that he himself, Tom, was the cutest thing on the beach. He liked the way his body had been changing lately. It was as if someone had been stealing into his bedroom every couple of nights with a basketball pump, sticking the needle part into his belly button, inflating his muscles. If this kept up, he'd be able to grate cheese on his belly.

Cute as he was, his perfectly cut hair, perfectly cool sunglasses, and perfectly fitting swimsuit that clung dangerously low on his hips were all wasted down here.

Tom sighed, feeling as if he were setting a world record for boredom. Without turning his head, he saw a young Mexican couple bobbing just beyond where the waves started to break. They weren't a whole lot older than he was—maybe two years, three max. Everybody in the water gave them lots of space. The boy wore a white T-shirt, the girl, a dark blue tank top. It was as if they'd dressed for a date and somehow ended up in the water and still didn't know they were all wet. Had they bothered to take off their shoes?

All Tom knew was that they'd been out there for an hour at least, holding each other so close fish couldn't swim between them, occasionally kissing, and constantly whispering in each other's ears. Didn't they ever get cold?

Tom almost felt sorry for them. The water wasn't very romantic or private. The guy probably didn't have a car. Maybe there were too many bugs and slithery things in the jungle a couple of blocks from the beach. Maybe . . .

Later, Tom would blame it on this kissy-kissy couple. If he hadn't been straining his eyes sideways to spy on them, he might have seen the soccer ball flying toward him.

It exploded against his cheek, knocking off his sunglasses, sending him partway off his reclining chair.

"Hey!" he bleated.

The sandy ball bounced off his face and landed a few feet away. A shadow spurted over the beach and Tom looked up to see a Mexican boy running toward him. The boy was smiling.

"*Gracias,*" he said, bending over to scoop up the ball.

Tom stared, still stunned, not knowing what to say.

Nodding once, the boy turned and ran back to his game. His naked back looked like sandpaper, except for the sweaty, clean curve of his spine. Also caked with sand, his jeans shone like wet paint under the grit.

Tom squinted against the sunlight and reached for his sunglasses. He was surprised they weren't broken. He blew sand off the lenses and gingerly slipped the glasses back on, his face smarting where the ball had hit.

Holding himself rigid, pretending that nothing had happened, Tom stared straight ahead, out into the bay. What had the boy said? *Gracias?* Thank you?

Tom reached up to wipe sand from his cheek. Had the boy thanked him for stopping the ball, or made fun of him for stopping it with his face?

He remembered the boy's smile—the too-white

teeth, the twinkling dark eyes. He blushed. No doubt about it, he thought, the boy had made fun of him.

Tom glanced to his right, wishing he could reach the shade and pull it over him. It now lay rumpled on the sand under a palm-thatched *palapa* that resembled a misshapen Asian-style hat on a stick. He swung his feet over one side, trying to decide if he had the energy to move his chair under the *palapa.* As he waited for inspiration, he dug his feet into the sand and lifted them, letting sand sift through his toes. He was surprised to feel something hard against the top of his right foot. A shell? A piece of broken bottle? It would be just like a Mexican beach to have dangerous junk hidden in the sand.

Bending over, Tom cautiously probed the sand with his hands. He carefully pulled something up. It wasn't glass or a shell. It was a twenty-peso coin.

Big and heavy as the coin felt, it was small change. But maybe there was more money lost where he was sitting—money fallen from purses or pockets over the years, disappearing from sight quick as hermit crabs. He dug his feet into the sand again, probing deeper and farther afield, then glanced over at the *palapa,* wondering if that might be a better place for treasure.

He didn't have any pockets, so he slipped the

twenty-peso coin into the pouch liner in the front of his swimsuit. He stood and the coin settled to the bottom of the pouch, feeling cool and heavy.

So this is what it feels like to be a man, he thought, grabbing the chair and dragging it. For the first time that morning, Tom let himself smile.

CHAPTER TWO

On the nightstand next to his bed, the twenty-peso piece seemed to wink. He couldn't believe it was the only coin in the sand, although it was the only one he'd found. What with winking money, pounding waves, a ceiling fan chopping chunks from the moon-milky light, and a snoring sister in the next bed, Tom was unable to sleep. He sat up and sighed.

Instinctively, he ducked his head as he walked under the fan. He had to admit that the wobbly, rattling thing helped some. It fluffed the hot air, keeping it from settling over his bed. Fluffed or heavy, the air was difficult to breathe. Like August in Minnesota, outside, at noon.

On his way toward the balcony, he wondered if he could reach as high as the rust-scabbed fan blades. He decided not to find out and looked at his sister instead.

Philippa was sleeping soundly, splayed diagonally

over her bed. The moonlight made her skin glow soft blue-white, which gave Tom the creeps. It was the color of dead people in the movies. He wondered if that was the color of death in real life.

He glanced above and behind her. It was still clinging to the wall: a little lizard. It was only a few inches long and white as the wall—a crescent moon with legs. It had been there since he'd gone to bed. Tom could make it out only by the faint shadow it cast. He'd been hoping it would drop down to his sister's bed and scurry over her, scaring her so much that she'd spend the night in their parents' room, next door.

One of the things he hated most about vacations was sharing a room. It meant that he was never alone. It meant that he couldn't escape being with the people he least wanted to be stuck with for the rest of his life. Prison must feel like this, he thought. He couldn't even brush his teeth without his sister barging in on him. And the door was so thin he never stood at the toilet, not wanting the splash of water to tell her what he was doing.

He looked at the sky. The moon was a little more than half full. Maybe someday he'd be able to vacation there. By himself. It was bound to be better than here. He'd play basketball with no gravity. Hit golf balls a mile. Get a moon-tan. Ogle cute chicks from Mars.

The moon seemed to rest on the tops of a small family of wild-haired coconut trees. Bats flitted across it, making it look as if it had fleas. Why not? In Mexico, everything looked as if it had fleas.

The beach below appeared deserted until he saw movement almost directly in front of him.

A man was standing knee-deep in the water, pulling in what looked like a rope. Tom had heard about drug smuggling up and down the western coast of Mexico and he wondered if this man was hauling in a stash of something that had been dropped off earlier by one of the decrepit fishing boats that wobbled around the bay.

Sure enough, a dripping blob came up from the water, and the man rummaged around in it for a few moments before straightening up.

Tom was excited that he might be watching something illegal. He crouched lower against the balcony's railing. What would they do if they saw him spying on this man? Who were "they," anyway? And this man? What was he doing?

The man shifted his haul to his right hand. He

stood still for a moment, as if listening to make sure he was alone. Then he flung out his arm under-handed. The bundle billowed from his hand, fanning out like a twirling skirt.

A fish net! The kind he'd seen in the pictures in an old illustrated Bible his parents kept in the study. The fishermen who became disciples of Christ had used round nets like this in the Sea of Galilee.

People still used that kind of net? The net landed softly on the water and sank from view. The man stood, waiting.

A dog came trotting along the sand and sat near the man. Tom recognized it. It had spent the day vis-iting everybody on the beach, never begging but getting a lot of attention and food anyway. Even Tom had given it a couple of potato chips. With dogs, you didn't need to speak Spanish to make yourself understood. Or liked.

He heard muffled noises coming from his room. Philippa tossing in her bed? Maybe the lizard had done its creepy-crawly thing.

He was startled instead to hear his mother's whisper. "Tom?"

"Yes," he whispered back, wishing he weren't in his underwear.

His mother stepped out from his room's doorway.

"You all right?" She was wearing a dorky T-shirt of his father's that hung to her knees.

He nodded, shielding his lap with folded hands. "Yeah. Couldn't sleep. That's all."

"I couldn't, either," she said, walking to the railing behind him.

He didn't say anything, even though it seemed that he should.

"What a beautiful night!" she said.

He nodded and then added, "Yeah." He tipped his head so that he could see the moon fleas jumping. The sound of waves seemed to measure the silence that followed.

"Are you having a good time?" his mother finally asked.

He heard in her voice the answer that she wanted. "Sure," he said, hoping to avoid a discussion.

He almost recoiled when she put a hand on his shoulder. "I'm glad. Your father and I have been wanting to share this place with you for such a long time. Life is so simple and beautiful here. So *basic*."

So boring, so stupid, so prehistoric, Tom wanted to say. He thought of the fisherman. So *biblical*. Instead of saying anything, he just nodded.

"Don't stay up too late," his mother said, lifting

her hand and moving toward the door. The air felt cool on the patch of skin where her hand had rested. She turned. "Remember, we're going into town tomorrow. We'd like to get an early start."

"Okay," he said. The town hadn't seemed like much when they'd driven through it from the airport. But it had to be more exciting than another day on the beach.

"Good night, sweetie."

"G'night," he mumbled and then settled back to spying on the beach.

The man and the dog were gone. Tom searched up and down the water's edge and saw them off to the left, not far, almost hidden by the night.

And then, from his right, he glimpsed the movement of somebody striding down the strip of hard sand that formed just beyond the water's reach. Tom saw it was a man. A soldier. In boots darker than the night sky.

He wore a cap with a small bill, shaped so that it made his head look like a box in the back. And he was carrying a rifle, swinging it casually from one hand in rhythm with his steps.

What was it his parents had said last night? That there seemed to be more soldiers now than they remembered? "I wonder if it means some kind of unrest?" his father had said, before he noticed Tom and Philippa were listening. He'd changed the subject.

Tom watched the soldier approach the fisherman, who was bringing his arm back, preparing to throw the net. His head snapped toward the soldier as his arm flew forward. Instead of forming a beautiful, dancing circle as it fell, the net crumpled and drop-ped into the water, a wave erasing its splash. The fisherman backed away from the soldier, into the waves, almost stumbling, almost sitting. Tom watched as the soldier bent over, picked something up off the beach, and tossed it toward the spot where the net had sunk. Arms hanging at his sides, stiff from fear or anger—Tom didn't know which—the fisherman watched the soldier turn and disappear into the foggy darkness farther down the beach.

For the first time that day, Tom felt chilled.

Soldiers. Fishermen from the Bible who might be drug smugglers. A moon with fleas. Lizards. When would the stars in the sky begin to move, rearrang-ing themselves to spell THE END in galactic block let-ters, telling him this nightmare was over?

Crouching as if he were sneaking from an R-rated movie before the lights came on, Tom returned to the room and threw himself facedown on his bed. He pulled the pillow around his head, heard the pounding of blood in his ears, regular as waves, irritating as the beating of the ceiling fan. The pounding slowed a little as his body relaxed.

He felt himself sinking into sleep when something scurried over his legs and up his bare back. He cried out before he could stop himself, and sat, clutching his pillow to his chest, searching the bed for the lizard.

His sister stirred and swallowed a snore as she lifted her head toward him.

"What's going on?" she asked sleepily.

He turned and flung the pillow behind him, against the wall. "Nothing," he answered, his whisper scraping against his throat, hating himself for being afraid, hating her for waking up. "Go back to sleep."

"Lizards don't bite, you know," she mumbled, yawning. And then, with a sigh, she rolled over and picked up snoring where she'd left off.

CHAPTER THREE

Tom imagined that he was attached to his parents and sister by hundreds of strings thin as spider webbing and strong as fishing lines. They were up ahead and he felt as if he were being tugged forward, his reluctant feet forced to move so he wouldn't fall flat on his face. Tiny, sharp grains of dried sweat were growing on the inside of his jeans, chafing him. His hair felt so much like the fake grass in Easter baskets that he was glad nobody back home could see him.

He squinted around, cursing himself again for forgetting his sunglasses. The walls surrounding some of the houses they walked by had bits of broken glass set in cement on top—what a nice, friendly decorating touch, he thought. Two- and three-story cement buildings on either side were cracked and stained under their film of white paint. Rusted lengths of twisty rebar stuck up above the top stories, as if the buildings' owners planned to add another story or two—undoubtedly to get above the exhaust-soaked heat and dirty fishbowl smells in the narrow streets where he was walking.

Without the continuous rumble of waves on sand, the city sounds were startling and clear. Old-fashioned VW Bugs whipped by, rattling as if they trailed lengths of chain. Birds didn't chirp. Instead, they sounded as if they were plunging their beaks into the tops of tin cans to get at what was inside.

As if that weren't weird enough, the conversations Tom heard in passing sounded like birds trying to speak like humans. How did these people understand each other?

What was wrong with his parents? They actually liked this place!

Tom looked disbelievingly at what the Mexicans around him were wearing. What Felicidad needed, he thought, was an army of fashion police. Instead, what they had were pretend police, men or women in crisp gray-green uniforms at nearly every corner, acting important, blowing whistles, waving white-gloved hands at traffic and pedestrians and maybe even God. And on the other corners there were very real soldiers—like the one he'd seen last night—with rifles slung over their shoulders. Some soldiers slouched against buildings. Others stood stiff and erect, moving nothing except their eyes—and maybe their fingers on their triggers—as they watched Tom passing. They gave him the creeps. Was something weird going on?

Every block or so there were a couple of buildings whose bottom spaces opened up onto the sidewalks like parking garages that were too small for cars. Shops of all kinds were crammed into these spaces.

Tom jammed his hands into the pockets of his jeans, avoiding the paper money his father had given him at breakfast—it was so damp with sweat now, it felt like used tissue. Instead, he grabbed the twenty-peso coin he'd found on the beach and fiddled with it. Not that he would spend it. He didn't see anything he wanted to buy. The clothes looked like rejects from his school's lost and found, even more pathetic since they appeared to have been washed and ironed. And every little grocery store looked like the rest, with their liquor bottles all lined up the same way. He'd walk past one and see the same strange brands of cigarettes, disposable diapers, and cooking oil that he'd seen in the last one.

Then, suddenly, he felt a sea breeze on his face. They'd turned onto a street bordering the town's beach and crowded with crude plywood stalls. The roughest-looking men, he decided, must be fishermen. Many sat in plastic chairs, already drinking beers, shouting conversations at each other while short, stocky women in faded dresses arranged fish on blood-darkened boards sparkling with fish scales.

Yet the street didn't smell fishy. Strange. And there weren't many flies.

Some of the fish were big and beautiful, fresh enough that their eyes weren't sunken yet. Some were as long as his arm, plump and showing bellies that almost glowed with luminous pinks and blues. Others were only several fingers in length and shiny as silverware.

He caught up with his family at one of the stalls.

"Ee-u-u-u!" Philippa squealed as they walked around it. "Look at this!"

The remains of a swordfish hung upside down on a chain attached to the branch of a tree. Even with the sword part chopped off, the fish was taller than Tom's father. Huge pieces of meat had been hacked away, exposing thin ribs as sharp as daggers.

"Imagine pulling this thing out of the water!" his father said, touching one of the ribs. He pulled back a finger covered with blood—not his own.

Tom walked around to the fish's other side, almost

stepping on something that shimmered and writhed. When his foot brushed by, a cloud of flies the size of a basketball rose from a pile of fish guts and rotated once before settling back on their feast. A fly convention.

"At least someone's eating this fish instead of stuffing it for a trophy," his mother said.

"We could charter a boat and do some sport fishing," his father suggested.

"Maybe next time," his mother replied.

Tom groaned. Next time? Not if he could help it. If he couldn't talk his parents into letting him stay with his best buddy, Henderson, he'd volunteer to keep Uncle Tucker from beer-drinking himself silly while he ice-fished. He'd promise to do—or not do— almost anything to escape coming back here.

"Ready for the market?" his father asked. Not waiting for an answer, he grabbed his wife's hand and struck off down a street that headed back into town, chanting: "To market, to market, to buy a fat pig!" He began to actually jiggedy-jig.

Tom held back, embarrassed, but kept his family in sight. The deeper they went into town, the more crowded their way became. Clogging the streets were more and more taxis, really small cars that didn't look like taxis, except for funny little taxi hats above their windshields. There were clumps of men pedaling big tricycles with huge baskets behind the seats and on the handlebars. The baskets were piled high with everything from fruit to mop handles.

Tom struggled to keep up with his family now.

"The market's just up there, Tom," his father called to him, pointing. "If we lose each other inside, let's meet back here in forty-five minutes."

Tom saw a sleek, modern-looking bank across the street and a stall on the corner selling comic books. By the look of the women on the covers, they weren't comic books for kids. Maybe he could ditch his parents right away and come back here to check them out while he waited.

"Sure," Tom said.

The market's entrance looked like an alley disappearing into a tunnel. There were stalls on either side, some open and some covered with awnings of canvas or wavy tin. People shouldered their way in both directions, going in and coming out. Tom didn't want to touch anyone, but in the crush he didn't have a choice. He wrinkled his nose. Somebody stunk. He was being pushed from behind and he pulled his hands from his pockets for balance, trying to tuck in behind his mother and father.

Tom couldn't tell where they were going. His

father turned a corner and stopped. Tom almost ran into him.

"Gosh!" his father exclaimed. "I'd forgotten. Look, honey! Let's try some."

They were standing at a stall where a girl about Tom's age was ladling milky water into plastic bags. She smiled at his father, took his money, and slipped a straw into the bag before twisting its neck and handing it to him.

Tom saw several kids gathered around this stall, grasping the twisted necks of their bags and sipping. They were staring at Tom and his family, looking shy as they drained what was inside, flattening the plastic.

"What is it?" Philippa asked, as she and Tom watched their father take a sip.

"Man!" he said, handing the bag to Tom's mother. "Just like I remember. It's curds and whey."

"Like Little Miss Muffet in Mother Goose?" Philippa asked.

"Yep," their mother said. Obviously not as enthusiastic as their father, she took a sip and handed the bag to Philippa, whose face was all scrunched up with hesitation. "See the lumps of curd on the bottom?" A shadowy white lump, like a decomposing goldfish, bounced through the milky liquid as

Philippa held it up to look at. "That's curdled milk . . . curds . . . the beginning of cheese."

"And the liquid . . . the whey . . . is the rest of the milk," their father added. "Full of protein. Really good for you."

"No thanks," Tom said, when Philippa tried handing the bag to him without tasting any herself.

"You don't know what you're missing," his father said, taking the bag from Philippa and sipping as he walked down a row of booths. He held his hand out to Tom's mother, who took it.

Thinking this would be a good time to lose them, thinking of the comic books outside, he let his parents and sister get several booths ahead before he turned and started walking back the way he'd come.

But nothing looked familiar. Had they passed these booths of fruit before? Or these vegetable stalls? He knew that they'd made one turn. Left or right? At a table of papayas, he turned to the right and immediately regretted it. He seemed to be going deeper into the market.

A wet smell wafted by, too powerful to ignore. He stopped to look. Sitting in a large, white plastic bucket was a pig's head. Just the head—snout up, mouth cracked open, notched ears cocked as if listening, stiff tongue looking as if the pig had been getting ready to lick its lips when the ax fell. The pig's eyes were open, blue, and looking as startled by Tom as Tom was by them.

Next to it was another bucket, full of glistening intestines. The bucket gurgled and shuddered as a bubble of gas broke through the guts, causing them to slide over each other.

The powerful, wet smell came again.

His heart quickening, Tom looked up and thought he saw his father's brownish head below a Santa-shaped piñata dangling from the eaves of a stall up ahead. He wove his way through people, trying not to bump into anybody. But when he got to the piñata, his family wasn't there.

CHAPTER FOUR

Tom took a deep breath, trying not to panic. He turned to face the stall he stood in front of, as if there might be answers in the dried fruit on display. All he saw were dates, prunes, and some things that looked like giant, freshly picked scabs. Something smelled perfume sweet.

Looking up, he noticed a boy standing several feet from him, staring at a pile of coinlike dried banana slices. It seemed impossible, but the boy looked familiar—like the same boy who'd thanked him for stopping the soccer ball with his head. Tom glanced over his shoulder to make sure. It couldn't be anybody else. The boy was walking behind him and the moment he saw Tom looking, he turned abruptly to study the dried beans one stall away.

Was the boy shadowing him?

Tom walked to the next stall and pretended to examine something that he didn't even recognize.

He looked sideways enough to see the boy move a stall closer, glancing at Tom carefully.

Tom eased his hands into the pockets of his jeans in case this boy was after his money. Tom sidled to the next stall, and, his hands pushing down so hard his jeans almost slid off, he leaned over some tiny peppers. He recoiled at their harsh smell. Glancing to the left, he saw that the boy had kept pace and was now touching a bag of dried something. A hand shot out from inside the stall and slapped the boy's hand. The boy grinned and said something to the hand's owner and looked over to see Tom looking at him.

The boy's smile disappeared, but only for a moment. Flashing Tom an even bigger smile, the boy approached him.

"You need help, amigo?" he asked. He seemed vaguely nervous around the eyes, but his smile was high voltage.

Tom frowned and turned without answering, craning his neck as he walked up the aisle, searching for his father's brown hair above the crowd. Every few steps he rose on tiptoe but didn't see anyone familiar. He fought an urge to see if the boy was still following. Yeah. The kid had guessed right. Tom did need help. But why had the kid been nervous speaking to him? It made Tom nervous to think the kid was up to no good.

Tom kept going, working his way toward the other side of the aisle. He hoped the boy wasn't following.

The smell of leather goods was strong, and he looked up at purses and belts hanging from a booth's canvas-draped ceiling. On a table below were several pairs of woven leather huaraches with soles cut from a car tire. These funny, monkey-footed shoes were the first things he'd seen in Mexico that he wanted to buy. Not only did they look cool, but nobody back home had a pair.

The woman sitting in the back of the booth smiled at him. She cradled a sleeping toddler in one arm.

He checked to see if he'd ditched the kid. He was relieved to see that the coast was clear. "How much?" Tom asked slowly, exaggerating the movement of his mouth. He pointed to the huaraches.

The woman nodded and said something in fast, birdlike Spanish.

Shrugging, Tom pulled the damp money from his pocket, trying not to tear it while flattening it, and showed her a hundred-peso bill. The woman shook her head and shifted her weight on her chair, careful not to jostle the toddler. She held up two fingers and then her eyes suddenly shifted from Tom to something behind him. Tom turned to see what she was looking at and found himself face-to-face with the boy.

"*Hola*," the boy said, his voice uncertain. "I am Ignacio." He waited for Tom to introduce himself. When Tom didn't, Ignacio turned toward the huaraches. "You want these?" He pointed.

Tom's eyes narrowed with suspicion.

"I will help," Ignacio said. "How much does she ask?"

"I think she says two hundred pesos," Tom answered, immediately cursing himself for taking Ignacio's bait.

Ignacio shook his head, looking sorry. "Too much."

Tom did the math in his head. Two hundred pesos seemed like a bargain. "Oh yeah?"

"*Sí*," Ignacio said. "You like them, I will help you." Before Tom could argue, the boy turned to the woman and spoke, gesturing toward Tom and the huaraches and then waving as if at something farther down the aisle.

The woman frowned and spoke, pointing to

Ignacio and Tom in a way that jarred her child. The
toddler whimpered and tried to nuzzle deeper into
her bosom.

Ignacio spoke again, his voice louder, his words
coming faster. The woman interrupted, her voice
higher and faster still. This wasn't an act. They were
angry with each other! They were fighting—causing a scene. Over him! Embarrassed, Tom looked
over his shoulder to see if anybody noticed. Several
people walking by stared at him.

"Forget it," he muttered, and turned to walk
away.

The woman stood, clutching the child to her.
"No, senor," she pleaded.

Ignacio touched Tom's arm. Before Tom could
tell him to get his mitts off, Ignacio leaned closer
and whispered, "She say . . . one hundred eighty.
There"—he pointed down the aisle—"one hundred
fifty. *Pero,* not so good."

"But two hundred sounds good to me!" Tom
blurted. He scowled at the huaraches and then at the
woman. The kid in her arms began to cry.

Ignacio made a face. "You will pay two hundred?"

Tom nodded. "If she has my size."

Ignacio asked the woman a question. She pretended to ignore him as she comforted her child. After a few moments she nodded.

"Here," Ignacio said, reaching for a pair and handing them to Tom. He knelt and began untying Tom's laces.

"Wait a minute, buster!" Tom shook his foot to keep Ignacio from fiddling with the laces. The shoe came off. He took a deep breath. What the heck. "That the right size? I take a nine."

Ignacio looked up, grinned, shrugged his shoulders, and slipped the huarache onto Tom's foot.

It fit. But then, the way its woven leather stretched to take on the shape of his foot, this shoe would probably have fit a duck.

Ignacio looked up. "You like?"

Tom stared at the shoe on his foot. It looked great. He rocked his foot back and forth. It felt great. Grudgingly, he nodded.

Ignacio stood and held out his hand. "The money," he said.

Tom handed him two hundred-peso bills. Ignacio handed them to the woman, who glared as she handed the boy back a twenty-peso coin.

Tom held out his hand for the change. Ignacio grinned and handed him the other huarache and his sneaker. "You pay two hundred pesos," he said brightly. And then, spinning around, he hurried away, dodging through people, disappearing.

It took a few moments for it to sink in. He'd been cheated out of twenty pesos! The woman, he saw, was trying to hide laughter behind her child's sleeping head. Of course, he'd been willing to pay two hundred pesos. Still. Tom thought of the coin that had lain undiscovered in the sand near the *palapa*. He was even now, but that didn't make him feel any better.

It hit him with the force of a soccer ball to the face. That kid—Ignacio—had made a fool of him again! His face burning almost as much as before, Tom hobbled from the stall with a huarache on one foot and a sneaker on the other.

"There you are!"

His father and mother smiled as they walked toward him, Philippa between them.

"We wondered where you'd gone," his father said. "It's almost siesta time. We've got to go before they start closing down these shops and the taxis get scarce for the afternoon."

His mother took the huarache from his hand. "These are nice." She smiled at him. "Nicer than the ones we saw back there." She tipped her head over her shoulder.

"How much did they cost?" his father asked.

"One-eighty," Tom said. It wasn't exactly a lie.

"Did you bargain the price down?"

Tom nodded. Avoiding her face, he took the huarache from his mother. He crouched, slipped off his other sneaker, and put on the new shoe. He tied the laces of his sneakers together and hung them around his neck.

Philippa stared at his feet in disgust. "They make you look like a Mexican."

"Philippa!" her mother scolded.

"If we could only stay another week, he'd be talking like one," his father said with a chuckle.

"Fat chance," Tom mumbled, but not loud enough for anybody to hear. Then he wondered how Mexicans would say it.

CHAPTER FIVE

Tom moved his beach chair so it faced away from the water. He lay on his stomach. His belly had gone from medium rare to well done. All it needed now was steak sauce. It was time to barbecue his baby-back ribs and his rump roast.

Only two more days to go before home.

What was the first thing he'd do when he got back to his own room? Get on the phone with his buddy Henderson or turn on the television? Tough choice. Maybe slip on his headphones or check his e-mail?

"To-o-om!" Philippa was panting as she ran up to him, kicking sand on his back. He lifted himself up on his arms and felt sand trickling down the crack of his butt. Even being careful, after a day at the beach toilet paper felt like steel wool. He didn't even want to think about what it would feel like now.

"Yeah?" he asked, his eyes narrow and mean.

Since Gordon had left for home yesterday, she'd been more of a pain than sand down the back of his suit. The only thing that saved her from his scorching eyes were his sunglasses.

"Mom and Dad want you to come eat."

"I'll be there . . . in a minute," he said, standing slowly.

"Okay!" Philippa said, running off down the beach.

He was hungry—really hungry. The only problem was food. Since being at the market in town yesterday, eating had been a problem. When Tom saw chicken on the menu, he pictured the plucked chickens he'd seen laid out side by side, their heads still on, their pimply skins bright yellow, eye-shaped stab wounds through their necks.

And hamburgers were out of the question. Even before the market, they'd been tough and tasted funny—as if leather had been ground in with the meat. But now, he pictured fly-covered strips of red meat that looked as if they'd been ripped off a still bellowing cow.

That left fish. Last week, if anybody had told him he'd be choosing to eat fish, he would have laughed in their faces. Not anymore.

Tom walked toward the restaurant, wondering

why the beach seemed different now from the week-end. There were fewer Mexicans and more Ameri-cans. Maybe that was it. There weren't boys playing soccer or kissy-kissy couples bobbing in the waves. There weren't fully dressed Mexican women loung-ing in the surf, heads toward the beach, dipping their fingers in the water and licking salt off them. Or barrel-chested Mexican men, looking as if they were hiding large cardboard boxes under the skin of their bellies, the top corners tucked under their ribs.

Instead, there were joggers and windsurfers and sunbathers. Americans were a lot less interesting to watch.

His parents waved as he approached. They seemed happy to see him. He tried to smile.

"Just in time to order," his mother said, grinning.

He should have taken off his sunglasses, but he didn't.

The waiter stepped up to the table. *"¿Cerveza?"* he asked Tom's father. Tom had noticed that the waiters never talked to his mother first if his father was with them.

"Sure. Why not?" his father replied. "We're on vacation. Do you want one?" he asked their mother. When she nodded, he turned to the waiter. *"Dos, por favor."*

"We're only on vacation for two more days," his mother said, sighing.

"Maybe I could call in sick," his father said, unwrapping his silverware from its diaper of napkin.

"Maybe *you* can. But *I* can't." Tom's mother turned to him. "Plus, I think Tom is ready to go back home."

True as it was, Tom felt embarrassed to admit it. He shrugged.

"What do you want to do this afternoon?" his father asked him.

Tom shrugged again.

"There's a nice beach we could go to around the point. We could hire a boat. Go snorkeling," his mother suggested.

Tom shook his head. Another beach? He was sick of waves and pelicans flying overhead with their necks that were kinked like a sink's drain pipe. He was sick of tasting saltwater in his mouth and feeling saltwater drying on his skin. "I want to go into town . . . find a couple of things to bring back."

His mother raised her eyebrows. He hoped she didn't suspect that he wanted to get something for Laura. And some dirty comics for Henderson. He'd have to go over the comics thoroughly—make sure they were a good value.

"Me, too!" said Philippa.

Horrified, Tom turned to her. "No!" he said.

His father grunted. "I think both of you would have a better time snorkeling. We can find some things at the airport to take back. Nobody will know the difference. Sure you don't want to come with us?"

It sounded as if his father was actually giving him a choice. Tom shook his head. "I'd rather go into town. One more time."

"Me, too!" said Philippa. She leaned over and whispered something in their mother's ear.

"I see," their mother said, smiling down at Philippa. "You can go, Tom. For a couple of hours. But you have to take your sister." She winked, to let Tom know there were secrets afoot. "She's going to look for something for me."

Philippa leaned over and pulled Tom's shoulder down. "Dad's birthday," she whispered into his ear loud enough to blow cobwebs out the other side. "It's next week!"

Tom groaned. Philippa and their mother beamed.

"What's with all the secrets?" their father asked, his eyes suspicious.

"Oh, nothing," said their mother in a singsong voice.

She winked again at Tom and then nodded, as if to say thank you.

"Well, I still think . . ." their father began.

"Let them go," their mother said, patting their father's hand. "It'll be an adventure."

CHAPTER SIX

Tom opened the back taxi door for Philippa, closed it, and then dived into the front passenger seat.

"*El zócalo, por favor,*" he announced to the taxi driver, using the phrase his mother had helped him practice. It would get them close to the market. His tongue felt weird from forming these foreign sounds, so he stretched it out, pushing it against his front teeth.

"Sure thing," the man said. "My name is Alejandro."

Tom blushed. Just his luck! The first time he screwed up his courage to speak Spanish it *would* be with a Mexican who knew English. And the guy didn't even have much of an accent.

Alejandro laughed, putting the taxi in gear. "You want to go to the plaza? Do some shopping and then go to the market?"

Tom nodded, his tongue suddenly shy.

Alejandro pulled out of the hotel's driveway and into traffic going to town. "You speak English?" he asked Tom, trying to sound serious. His smile betrayed him as he settled into his seat, draping his left arm out the window.

"Yes," Tom managed to say. "And you . . ."

"My sister lives near Los Angeles. In Orange County. I lived with her for a couple of years, you know, working for her husband."

"Yeah?" Tom searched his brain for something to say and pounced on the first thing. "What'd you do?"

"Worked on cars. Where you from?"

"Minnesota. Minneapolis."

"You go to any Twins games?"

"A couple of times," Tom lied. He'd never been to a major league baseball game in his life. He thought baseball was boring, that it could be improved with tackling or exploding balls. His father used to ask him to go and had finally given up.

"I'm a Dodgers fan," Alejandro said.

"Oh." Tom didn't know for sure what city they were from. He looked out the window at the ugly cement buildings whizzing by. He saw a clump of people standing around what looked like a bus stop. They made waiting look as easy as watching television. To

Tom it would have been like watching a blank screen. A block from there, he saw a couple of soldiers walking on the sidewalk, going toward town. On the next block, there were a couple more.

He turned to the driver. "Why did you come back? Here?"

"This is where my wife and my children live. And my father and mother." He shrugged. "Here, I grew up, with my neighbors. There . . ." He shrugged again and smiled. "And I brought back this car."

Tom tensed as a beat-up VW taxi cut in front of them so close he was sure they'd crash. Alejandro honked and leaned out his window. Tom was surprised when Alejandro laughed and waved. The VW's driver leaned out the window and looked back, smiling as if he'd just done something clever.

"What's going on?" Philippa shouted, so close to Tom's ear it hurt. She clung to the back of the front seat.

"My brother-in-law," Alejandro said, and shrugged again.

"Oh," said Philippa. "Why didn't you tell us to wear seat belts?"

Alejandro grinned at her over his shoulder. "Don't have none."

"Why not?"

Alejandro shrugged. "With me driving, you don't need them. Besides," he said, motioning to a small, plastic statue that was glued to the dash, "with *Nuestra Senora de Guadalupe,* you are safe."

"Who is she, anyway?" Tom asked. She looked saintlike. A halo of flames shot out all around her, from her head to her feet. Yet she was smiling. Tom hoped Alejandro didn't belong to some fanatical religious cult that involved gasoline and a match.

"Nuestra Senora de . . ." Alejandro paused. "In English? Of course. Our Lady of Guadalupe. She's the patron saint of *México.* Just like the Virgin Mary is the mother of *Jesús,* Our Lady of Guadalupe is the mother of *los indios . . .* the Indians, and the Catholics, here in *México.*"

"How did she get to be a saint?" Philippa asked, leaning over the front seat.

As Alejandro explained about an Indian peasant named Juan, and the hill and the roses flowering in winter, and the miracle of the cloak, Tom wished he was wearing a seat belt. Alejandro was so caught up in telling his story that he didn't seem to pay much attention to driving. Tom imagined himself impaled on the statue, wearing the windshield around his neck.

He was relieved when they pulled up to *el zócalo.*

". . . and so, on that hill, today, is a big church for Our Lady," Alejandro proudly concluded.

"That's a great story," Philippa said. "Is it true? About the roses?"

Alejandro smiled. "Yes. It is."

"Thanks," Tom said, handing Alejandro the money he'd counted ahead of time and had been holding in his hand.

"*Gracias,* senor," Alejandro said grandly as Tom opened the door. "See you around."

The plaza was nothing more than a cement square with basketball hoops at either end. On either side of it were steps going from the street to the court, where people were smoking, talking, eating ice cream, or doing nothing at all. Beyond *el zócalo* was a beach with gray sand blending into gray water.

Everyone here was Mexican. Even though nobody stared, or even seemed to notice them, Tom felt strange. There was a clump of soldiers standing at one end of the basketball court, watching a handful of boys without shirts shooting baskets, showing off for a half-dozen girls.

"Let's go over there." Tom pointed to their left. "That's the way to the market," he said, trying to look as if he knew.

The sidewalk soon narrowed and they found

themselves walking in front of booth after booth filled with artsy-craftsy silver jewelry, piñatas, blankets, and onyx carvings of animals.

"Hey, look!" Philippa called, when they got to a booth jammed with the kind of embroidered white dresses that some of the Mexican women and girls wore. She tugged at Tom, pulling him into the booth.

The dresses were hung so high and close together that Tom couldn't turn without one brushing his face. A woman appeared from somewhere, smiling at Philippa.

"Oh-o-o! This one has animals on it!" Philippa said, pointing. The woman lifted it down on a forked stick for her to see. "I want it!" His sister held the dress up to herself. It was a match.

"How much?" Tom asked the woman.

"*Sesenta,*" she said.

Before Tom could say anything, Philippa said, "I'll take it!" She handed the woman the bills their father had given her. The woman leafed through them quickly and looked up. "*Diez más,*" she said.

"More?" Tom asked. The woman nodded. He looked at Philippa and shook his head. "Look. I'm not going to spend *my* money on a dress."

The woman was watching them closely. When

Tom finished, she offered the money back to Philippa, who hesitated before reaching out to take it. Tom saw her fingers trembling slightly and that her mouth was trembling, too.

She was going to cry. Quickly he took money from his own pocket. "You don't have to cry about it," he said. "Here."

She just looked at him, as if she couldn't believe what he was doing. He could hardly believe it himself.

Looking at the woman, he asked, "How much more?"

She held up all ten fingers. He shook his head and held up five fingers. She hesitated, looked at Philippa, and shook her head. Tom felt skunked. She knew that he'd pay ten to keep his sister from making a scene. He handed the woman a ten-peso coin and she slipped the white dress into a tissue-thin plastic bag and handed it to Philippa.

Philippa threw her arms around Tom's waist. "Thanks," she said to his belly button.

"Don't get all mushy on me . . . Filly."

She pushed away from him and smiled. "You haven't called me that for . . . forever."

He grunted but couldn't help smiling.

"Thanks," he said over Philippa's head, toward

the lady. They left the booth and headed up the street, where he hoped the market would be. It felt good, holding Philippa's hand.

They passed the booth of adult comics. There was a boy about his age standing in front of it, thumbing through one, his eyes jumping every couple of seconds to see who was looking at him. Tom wished he could have stopped, but, with his sister tagging along, he would have too much explaining to do.

The market's entrance seemed even more crowded than before. With his free hand, Tom shoved his sunglasses to the top of his head, to see better in the dim light. He eased Philippa into the current of people going in. Tom steered her with a hand on her shoulder, hoping they weren't headed toward the booths of pig heads and plucked chickens.

They passed the booth where he'd bought his huaraches. He wasn't wearing them now—he'd worn them so much that first day that they'd made a blister on his left heel. As they walked past fruits and vegetables and candies, Tom kept a lookout for Ignacio. He didn't want the kid to make a fool of him in front of Philippa.

They approached a booth with painted wooden masks, and Tom pulled back on Philippa's shoulders, stopping her. The masks looked like the faces of devils and monsters and catlike beasts that were only part human. They weren't pretty but they had personality. Attitude. He liked that. Walking into the booth, he looked at the mask of an angel that looked as if it were on the verge of throwing up.

"What do you think?" he asked Philippa.

"Gross," she said, sounding impressed.

"Think Henderson would like it?"

She nodded enthusiastically.

Next to the angel was the mask of a snarling cat. He lifted it off its nail and held it up to his face, growling as he looked at Philippa. She giggled.

A familiar voice came from behind. "You like?"

Tom froze. Slowly, turning around, he slid the mask from his face. Ignacio was sitting on a stool in the corner of the booth. A textbook was opened on his lap, as if he were doing homework. An older man, who looked like his father, sat beside him, his head tipped back, sleeping.

"Fifty pesos," Ignacio said, not waiting for Tom to answer.

Tom put the mask back on its nail and took Philippa's hand. The guy already had twenty pesos that belonged to him.

"They come from the mountains around my village," Ignacio said. "The one you hold, it is a jaguar. The one next to it is *un perro*. A dog."

Before Tom could say something insulting, a nearby woman began to shout. She sounded both scared and angry.

All around, people started moving nervously, scurrying. Tom saw two soldiers pound past the booth, breathing hard, green uniforms stained with sweat, guns held against their chests. Tom grabbed Philippa and pulled her farther into the booth.

From the corner of his eye, he saw that Ignacio's father was awake now, his eyes dark, both worried and irritated.

Another soldier ran by shouting.

"*Nuestra Senora . . .*" Ignacio gasped at the sound of gunfire.

A child screaming caused Ignacio to drop to the ground. Tom and Philippa joined him. The boy's father snorted and stood. "*Idiotas,*" he grunted. Deliberately, almost slowly, he began taking masks off the walls and tossing them into a box by his feet.

A burst of gunfire made his eyes narrow as he looked at Tom and Philippa. Shifting his gaze to his son, he said, "*Ven acá,*" and pulled open the canvas flaps in the back of the booth, keeping his eyes on Ignacio.

The popping of more gunfire made Tom cringe. "What's going on?" he asked Ignacio, who looked as frightened as Philippa, as frightened as Tom felt.

Ignacio's father growled and shook the canvas opening. Tom's father had never once growled like that. The thought of his father filled Tom with a longing to be with his parents.

"Come," Ignacio said, instead of answering. His lips were white from pressing them together. He ducked under his father's arm. Herding Philippa, Tom crawled through the gap, into an alley between Ignacio's booth and the booth behind it. Bursts of gunfire were steady now and seemed to be spreading throughout the market. Tom heard the ping of metal hitting metal. Men and women were shouting and children were crying. The three of them hurried along the alley behind Ignacio's father, who was pushing and kicking his box ahead of him.

Where the alley opened onto a wide aisle, Tom saw women running, bent over, herding children. He saw crouching men lurch from booth to booth, like kids playing soldier. One of them had a rifle. And he wasn't wearing a uniform. He raised the rifle to his shoulder when, suddenly, his head snapped back and blood spurted from his neck. He crumpled to the floor, his legs twitching.

Fear seized Tom's body, making it impossible for him to move.

Philippa turned to him. Tom was glad she hadn't seen the man being shot. "We're going to be all right," she said, her voice bossy. She reached for his hand and tried to pull him toward her.

When he didn't budge, she pulled again, harder. The movement unlocked his mind. His heart began to race, and his hands and legs scrambled to catch up with it. He looked ahead and didn't see Ignacio or his father. "Hey, wait!" Philippa squeaked.

"Here," Tom whispered. He crawled under a table, next to a tooled belt with a saucer-sized buckle that lay on the floor. The gunfire and shouting seemed to have moved away. Tom wondered what would happen if somebody found them. Surely the soldiers or the people with the guns wouldn't dare to kill two American kids. Would they?

Philippa crawled closer. The crinkle of her plastic bag seemed incredibly loud. She climbed into the nest of his lap and sat, clutching the bag. It felt good to put his arms around her. It kept him from shaking so badly. He smelled her hair, which was pressed up against his face. It didn't smell of shampoo, but of the detergent for washing clothes in the sink. She'd accidentally used it this morning.

He wondered what they should do. Stay put until everything seemed safe? Ignacio and his father were probably long gone, on their way to the mountains where the masks came from. And who could blame them? Why should they risk their lives for two American kids?

Tom gasped as somebody ran toward the table. A pair of boots clumped by. Soldier boots and legs cut off from view. Philippa tensed and Tom held her tighter.

For a moment there was silence, as if the market were holding its breath. Tom strained to listen and heard nothing but the slow flapping of a cloth somewhere. And then from his right he heard a hiss.

He turned to see Ignacio, who beckoned them with frantic, jerky motions.

CHAPTER SEVEN

Philippa scrambled off Tom's lap. Without her weight, Tom felt as if he were rising from the floor. He lunged onto his hands and knees and followed Philippa and Ignacio around a corner. Tom felt the roughness of cement as the cloth gave way in the right knee of his jeans.

They skittered around a shaft of light that came from a hole in the ceiling and dodged several up-turned tables and scattered goods—silver chain brace-lets and straw hats and T-shirts and a tangle of Barbie-like dolls. A scream came from behind them, and sounds like someone beating on a pillow. Ignacio stood, hunched, and ran. Tom began to sprint and almost tripped over Philippa, who had fallen. He reached out his hand to help her up.

She scrambled to her feet, ignoring Tom's out-stretched hand, and began running. He noticed the plastic bag with the dress only after he'd passed. He wasn't about to go back.

Ahead of them was a door so small that Tom had to duck his head to run through it. The sun's brightness hit him as if he'd run out of a movie theater in the middle of the afternoon. He groped the top of his head, searching for his sunglasses. They were gone.

Tom squinted and saw a truck shaking and wheezing in front of them, its passenger door open. Ignacio's father was at the wheel. Ignacio scrambled inside, straddling the gearshift. He beckoned them frantically. Tom helped his sister into the truck and climbed in after her.

The truck lurched forward, jerking around corners, tires squeaking quietly. Jets of dirt shot up through holes in the floor.

Something hit the windshield, jarring Tom's ears with a sound like ice being chewed. A spiderweb of cracks instantly appeared. Ignacio's father slammed on the brakes, rolling Ignacio into Tom and Philippa. The truck began to skid, and, at the same time, the man gunned it.

He drove as if the steering wheel were trying to jerk itself from his hands. Tom clung to the seat, three fingers of his right hand hooked through a hole in the upholstery. The door to his right chattered. He hoped it wouldn't pop open. He clenched his teeth, straining to see through the cracked windshield, wondering if the bumps he felt were the truck going over potholes or running over dogs or even people. He put an arm around Philippa's shoulders to keep her from flopping into him.

They rode like this for many frantic minutes until the truck began to slow. Tom looked sideways and saw Ignacio's father leaning close to the steering wheel, as if he had finally tamed it. Looking out of the passenger window, Tom saw that they were no longer in the thick of the town.

And from the direction they were going in— toward the hills—Tom realized suddenly that they were headed away from the hotel.

He turned to Ignacio. "The hotel. My parents are back there!"

The boy shook his head and jerked his thumb over his shoulder. Tom twisted to look out the back window.

Flames were licking at a huge cloud of smoke, black and boiling from town. Tom shifted his gaze to where the hotel should be and saw more smoke.

The blood seemed to drain from his heart. "We've got to go back!" he cried. Philippa grabbed his hand.

Ignacio spoke to his father, the words coming

quickly. His father said something in return. The boy turned back to Tom. *"Peligroso . . .* what do you say . . . dangerous! Men fighting. *Y"*—his fingers waved—*"¿qué dice? . . .* fire!" He shook his head again. "At our village, you will be safe."

Didn't this kid understand how important it was for them to go back? Tom felt tears sting his eyes. "Look . . ." he began, when he remembered. His parents had taken a boat to some beach or other. They were probably facedown, waves breaking over their bottoms, ogling fish and sea plants that could have been colored by a kindergartner. They probably didn't even know anything had happened in Felicidad.

Philippa looked up at him. "What about Mom and Dad?"

"They're okay. Remember? They went snorkeling." It felt good to say. Philippa considered what he'd said a moment and then nodded.

Tom glanced at Ignacio. His parents had always warned him about hitchhiking, about trusting strangers. Could Ignacio and his father be trusted? Why had Ignacio come back for the two of them? Why had Ignacio's father waited in the truck when he was in danger, when he could have gotten away sooner? Was this more than kindness? Did they think there might be money it in?

After all, Ignacio had cheated him out of twenty pesos.

Tom felt Philippa crying before he heard her. He looked down and saw a large tear sliding down her cheek. Her face was pinched tight to keep more tears from coming. Putting his arm around her shoulder, he pulled her against him. "I told you." He struggled to sound soothing. "Mom and Dad are all right. You just wait and see."

Philippa shook her head. "My dress!" Her voice was full of anguish. "I lost my dress!" She grabbed his chest and hugged.

"Geez, Philippa! There are more important things than stupid dresses to . . ." He stopped himself, hugging her back. "We'll get you another one, Filly," he said to the top of her head. "Just like it. Maybe even better."

After a few moments, she began to relax her hold on him, which helped to calm him, too.

"Your sister?"

Tom looked at Ignacio and nodded. "Philippa," he said.

The boy nodded. "And you?"

"Tom."

"T-ahm," the boy said, smiling.

The father spoke to the boy and glanced at Tom,

almost shyly. The boy turned to Tom. "My father is called Diego. He asks what your father is called."

"Fred."

Ignacio nodded and reached out his hand, inviting Tom to shake it. Tom took it. "Thanks for helping us, Ignacio."

"No problem," Ignacio said, grinning—the same grin Tom remembered from the beach.

Tom looked at Ignacio's father, who was looking at him instead of the road. "Thank you, sir," he said. The man nodded.

Ignacio put a finger to his lips and tipped his head toward Philippa.

Tom looked. How could she sleep at a time like this?

CHAPTER EIGHT

The road began to climb between folds in hills that seemed as rumpled as a trashed, sweaty bed on Saturday morning. In town the road had been pavement, much of it cracked and uneven. Since they'd left town it had disintegrated into dirt and potholes.

Steep hillsides leaned like cliffs that were being pushed over by the weight of the sky. The road was cluttered with rocks that had rolled off them. Some of the trees clinging to the hills were no more than gnarled posts with huge crowns of tangled, thorny nests. Other trees had flowers. Bursts of white and red, but mostly yellow, seemed trying to escape the foliage. Among these trees were patches of tall, skinny cactuses and bushes with large leaves. The trees belonged in a jungle, the cactuses belonged in the desert, and the bushes belonged in a doctor's waiting room. It was a strange combination.

Ignacio's father jerked the truck to the other side

of the road and Tom glimpsed a lone burro with delicate hooves who flicked his ears backward in annoyance as they passed.

Up ahead, near the road, he saw a tree covered with red flowers. As they got closer, the flowers sprouted wings and flew off in an explosion of color. Spellbound, Tom watched as the birds spiraled upward, disappearing into the sky.

"Did you see that?" He turned to Philippa. Her eyes were still closed, popping open only when the truck hit a bump. She nuzzled her face into his shirt and sighed.

Ignacio was smiling at him. He put his hands on top of the gearshift knob, as if it were a cane and he were a gentleman. "You and your sister will be safe. With *mi familia*."

Tom let his head nod with the truck bumps. Visions of flowering birds were replaced by visions of people in the market running helter-skelter, of soldiers running, of red spurting from one man's neck. He shuddered and looked out the window. As the road curved to the left, the hill fell away to his right. Tom found himself staring into a deep valley. There was no shoulder. The truck swerved again to avoid a large gash in the road, as if a monster had taken a bite of it, leaving rocky crumbs behind.

Tom had never had a problem with car sickness. Until today. The truck began to thrash one way and the other as the road snapped back and forth, following the curve of the hills. His mouth watered and he kept swallowing sour fumes that rose from his stomach. It helped him feel better to stare around the cracked windshield, to the road ahead.

He saw what looked like a knitted wool cap with pipe-cleaner legs walking across the road. A tarantula? Tom struggled not to disturb Philippa as he twisted enough to look over his shoulder. The spider was now a flattened spot in the dirt.

And then, suddenly, the road grew worse. The truck shuddered and rattled. Tom held his sister more tightly and she snorted, sitting up with a start. Ignacio's father pumped the brakes several times, slowing the truck as they went over a speed bump that was made from a narrow tree trunk sawed in half lengthwise and laid, rounded side up, across the road. Out his window, Tom heard the flat side of one end slapping against the ground.

The village they entered was small, a few shacks scattered here and there, some close together and some by themselves, some with thatched roofs and some with tin. Tom kept hold of Philippa as she sat up on her knees to see better out the window. Her head swiveled as they passed a naked boy standing by the road. The boy's black hair fell over his forehead like tent flaps blowing open, and his eyes stared out as if from a hiding place. He held a piece of twine that was tied to the front leg of a puppy. The puppy was fighting the string, rear legs dug in, tail up, ears down.

Beyond the boy were two women carrying loads of something in light blankets that were slung over their foreheads and hanging down their backs. The women walked tall and looked straight ahead. They were barefoot and their white dresses were smudged with red dirt where their hands brushed back and forth.

Ignacio's father leaned on the horn. An enormous pig was walking toward them, right down the middle of the road. The pig didn't move, and, muttering something that sounded like curses, the man jerked the truck to the left at the last minute. Tom looked at the pig as they went by and saw it was a sow, its gigantic teats hanging almost low enough to plow dirt.

The road began to climb. In a sudden cleft Tom saw mountains beyond the hills. They were dark and yellowish, almost like the rotting teeth of the neighbor's old, almost-blind, totally deaf dog back home. As the truck climbed away from the village, they passed a couple of large patches of hillside that were covered in tall grass and reminded Tom of green scribbled in a coloring book. Other patches were covered in stalks of corn, with yellow tassles like the ones on toothpicks.

Ignacio's father turned to the left once more. Tom braced Philippa and himself as they plunged into the forest, following ruts that disappeared into a crease between two hills, and then climbed onto a saddle between them. As they started down the other side, Tom saw a village below, sitting in a wide valley. In the center of the thatched roofs was a whitewashed church, the tile on its roof the same red color as the dirt all around.

"La Esperanza," Ignacio said, with a big smile. "My family's *ranchito* is there." He pointed beyond the village and to the right.

As they approached the village, Philippa turned to Ignacio. "How come you speak English?"

Tom had wondered the same thing, but, unlike his sister, he hadn't had the nerve to ask.

"My father's brother, he went to *el norte,* to Colorado. He lives in Felicidad now and *mi padre y yo,* we live with him when we are there. He teach me. And"—he smiled—"I sometimes see American *programas* on *televisión.*"

"Cool," Philippa said. Tom found himself feeling jealous that Ignacio could use both English and Spanish. Tom had always thought taking a second language in school was a waste of time. Not now.

La Esperanza was bigger than the village with the naked boy. Nobody was walking along the road or riding bikes. Was it siesta time? There seemed to be many people sitting in the shade of buildings and trees, staring without interest as they passed by.

The truck made a sharp turn and then picked up speed.

Philippa bounced on the seat, twisting and turning as if she were trying to look out all the windows at once. "When will we be at your house?" she asked.

"*En un ratito,*" Ignacio answered.

"Is that soon?" Philippa asked.

Ignacio nodded.

The road was so narrow that it was canopied by trees. The power poles they passed weren't spaced evenly, and the lines strung between them looked stretched out and flabby from holding back the branches. Flickering sunlight and patchy shadows made the windshield seem to blink as the truck drove between two whitewashed stone pillars, a rusty iron arch spanning them. Welded into the arch, in block letters, was the word CARDENAS.

"This your family's ranch?" Tom asked.

Ignacio nodded, looking proud.

"Your last name is Cardenas?" He hoped he was pronouncing it halfway right.

Ignacio shook his head. "No. Senor Cardenas, my mother's uncle, he is dead. My family, *los* Guerreros, we have lived here for twenty years. Now, it is ours."

Beyond the gate were trees, here and there, with white-painted trunks and strange, globby fruit. Grass and weeds grew among the trees. The road seemed to open up, and, ahead, Tom saw a clump of short palms. The light on their leaves was silver. A puff of air made them shiver in a way that made them look, for a moment, like water spouting.

Past the palm trees was a collection of buildings that seemed to be sinking into the ground. All of them had thatched roofs except one, whose roof was even more red than that of the church in La Esperanza. As they drove closer, Tom saw that the roof was not made of tile, but was covered with small red peppers.

A skinny dog bolted toward them, barking. Chickens squawked and flapped, scattering. Several small pigs ran squealing from the truck. A goat sprang away.

A girl ran toward the truck from the building with the pepper roof. Senor Guerrero opened his door and stepped out. The girl ran into his arms, crying, "¡Papi! ¡Papi!"

Suddenly the truck was surrounded by children. A couple of shrieking, laughing faces bobbed up and down outside the passenger window, trying to look in. A naked boy, about three or four, was hopping, trying to grab the passenger door handle, but he was too short to reach it.

Tom felt a gentle elbow against his ribs. "We must get out," Ignacio said.

The hinges popped as Tom reached over Philippa and opened the passenger door. He helped his sister down and then stepped down himself, feeling shy. Once on the ground, Philippa clung to his leg.

The children became suddenly quiet. The naked boy stepped back and stared at them. In an important-sounding voice, Ignacio said, *Americanos. El niño se llama Tom. La niña, Filipa.*"

Tom smiled as if he were hiding gum in his mouth from a teacher. "Hi," he said, through clenched teeth.

A girl about Philippa's age covered her mouth with the back of her hand and giggled. A boy a couple of years younger than Ignacio walked over to Philippa, a huge smile on his face. He held a yellow chick in his hands and offered it to her.

Tom felt her grip loosening. He was about to warn her of fleas and whatever else people got from unclean animals when she let go and took the chick in her own hands. "It's so cute!" she said. The other children gathered around her, all of them talking at once.

"You like horses?" Ignacio asked Tom. The boy walked toward what looked like a fence, except that it was made of postlike cactuses that were nearly as high as he was.

Tom hesitated. He looked at his sister. "You okay, Filly?"

She looked up at him and laughed. "It tickles!"

Tom saw that the chick was pecking at her palms.

"You want to hold it?" she asked, offering the chick to him.

"Naw. Maybe later," he added, wanting to leave no doubt that it wasn't because he was afraid. He turned quickly and followed Ignacio toward the cactus fence.

CHAPTER NINE

Tom was afraid of horses. They were too big and they tossed their heads and they had dangerous-looking hooves. But the horse in front of him was almost too ugly to fear. Its legs splayed out like those of a sawhorse. Its hide was covered in patches that looked like mold.

Ignacio had his face buried in the horse's neck and was scratching in the hollow V under its jaws. The horse just stood, as if it didn't know what else to do, and stared at Tom. Tom stared back. He didn't remember horses having such broad foreheads or such large chins with so many sharp-looking hairs, thick as wire.

The horse's ears flicked back and it batted its head down, nipping at Ignacio's shirt. Ignacio responded by slapping its jaw and laughing. The horse's head bobbed a few times, as if the animal expected another slap, but it held its ground.

"What's his name?" Tom asked, keeping a safe distance.

Ignacio shrugged. "He's just *un caballo* . . . a horse."

Without warning, Ignacio grabbed a hank of mane on the bump at the base of the horse's neck and jumped, pulling himself on top. The horse danced a moment and snorted. Ignacio leaned over and whispered something into one of the horse's cocked ears. To Tom's surprise, the horse stopped dancing.

And then, slick as water, Ignacio slid off to stand in front of the horse, hands on his hips. He spoke to the animal in Spanish, his voice staccato, his words snapping with hard sounds. The horse listened for a few moments, turned around, and walked away.

Ignacio laughed and turned to Tom. "Tom," he said, "do not tell a horse you love him. He will not give you respect again." Grabbing his nose with his thumb and forefinger, Ignacio blew into his cupped hand. Tom flinched as Ignacio flicked the glob on his hand to the ground and then wiped the shininess on his jeans. "Come. *¿Tienes hambre?* You have hunger?"

The dog was waiting for them outside the cactus fence. He was as skinny and as ugly as the horse, in a doggy kind of way. His ribs looked like ropes

wound around his chest, straining to hold it together. His tail twitched, as if he were uncertain
about wagging it. He kept just out of kicking range,
but trotted along beside them, head cocked so that
he could watch both Ignacio and where he was
going. A pig joined the procession, as plump under
its skin as the dog was lean. Behind the pig came a
chicken. Tom felt silly to be part of such a parade.

They were aiming toward the building with the
red pepper roof. Smoke squeezed out from its peak,
then drifted down, making the peppers seem to
smolder. He heard children laughing inside.

Ignacio grunted something to the dog and pig.
He halfheartedly kicked out. They shied from him,
the chicken flapping its wings to go backward. Tom
ducked as he followed Ignacio under the low eaves of
the porch and through a doorway.

He stepped into a hot and smoky room. Daylight
barely penetrated the curling smoke that rose from a
fire under a griddle on rocks in the middle of the
floor. To one side of the griddle sat a large iron pot
on a grate, bubbling up a wonderfully rich smell.
Kneeling at the other side of the griddle was a
woman who looked up from what she was doing and
smiled at Ignacio and Tom. "M'ijo," she said to
Ignacio, beckoning with her hands. Ignacio knelt in

front of her and she gave him a hug. She smiled again at Tom before turning back to the fire.

Not knowing what else to do, Tom stood where he was, breathing in the rich, humid smells of cooking food. He made out a smell like popcorn popping and something else that must have been a stew. He looked beyond Ignacio's mother and saw the round faces of children take shape in the darkness as if they were developing in an instant photo.

He was relieved to hear his sister's voice. "Sit down, silly," she said, her blond hair nearly glowing in the dim light. "The momma is making some tore-*tea*-uhs." She said the Spanish word slowly and then smiled at her success.

Tom knelt, watching as the mother pinched off a bit of dough from a large lump that sat in a bowl next to her. She rolled it into a ball and then pressed her hands together, smashing it. She began slapping the dough with one hand and then the other, the thin pale disk twirling and growing between her hands. When she flicked it onto the griddle it looked like a large hole shot into the dark metal. After a few seconds, she flipped it over with her fingers, waited, and then plucked it off the griddle with one hand. With her other hand, she lifted a cloth covering a nearby basket and dropped the tortilla on top of a stack.

It was like magic, the way she made the dough grow between her hands as easily as spilled milk spread. Tom could have watched longer, but after she had made three more, the mother spoke to Ignacio and handed him the basket of tortillas.

Ignacio smiled and beckoned to Tom. "We go find my father," he said.

The dog and pig were waiting for them outside the cooking hut. They were arranged in the same order as before: The pig followed the dog and the chicken followed the pig. Farther off was a goat. Tom liked the look of its beard.

Ignacio said something sharp to them, once more kicking out. The dog slid out of the way, but the pig was not so lucky. As it scrambled away, squealing, it dumped a load of poop. The chicken pounced. Tom walked around it but noticed that there were bits of undigested seeds—corn mostly—in what the chicken was pecking.

"Come!" Ignacio called happily. Tom trotted to catch up.

They walked into a scrubby forest. Everywhere he turned, Tom saw skinny trees and spindly bushes and patches of weedy ground cover. Here and there were cactuses whose branches looked like green Ping-Pong paddles stuck together. Ignacio swept his arm in a grand, all-encompassing gesture. There were several bushy trees with enormous leaves that seemed snipped at by a child with scissors. "We grow banana and papaya. And that," he said, pointing to a low spikey bush, "is a *piña* . . . a pineapple." Tom saw in the middle a miniature, green waxy knob shaped like a pineapple that looked as if it were melting.

"A baby one?" Tom asked.

"*Sí,*" Ignacio said, handing him the basket of tortillas.

Ignacio went to a tree that looked like a locust but had large, fuzzy bean shapes hanging from it. Ignacio picked one and pulled a pocketknife from his jeans. "This is *tamarindo,*" he said. He cut a wedge from the fruit and handed it to Tom. He cut off another and popped it into his mouth.

Hesitating, Tom nibbled a corner. It was softly tangy and more complicated than a mouthful of different kinds of jelly beans. Was it lemon he tasted, or apple? Or was it root beer?

"Good?" Ignacio asked, his voice encouraging.

Tom grunted, nodding, wanting to spit it out.

"Is good in water. Like *limonada.*"

Tom nodded as Ignacio smiled and handed him another slice before continuing into the forest. Tom tucked in behind him, flicking the fruit off to the side and quietly spitting out the wad in his mouth.

Birds called from every direction, some high and some low, some angry and some singing, but all of them loud and unruly. Among the birdcalls Tom heard clicking noises and rustlings that made him jumpy.

"Do you have any bad-ass critters around here?" he asked. "You know, snakes or things?"

"Yes," Ignacio answered. *"Víboras.* What do you call . . . these?" He wagged his finger, making a hiss-rattle sound.

"Rattlesnakes?"

"Sí."

"Snakes that"—he made sucking noises—"from cows. At night, sometimes, they come where we sleep and drink the milk from our mothers." He held his arms to his chest, as if cradling a baby. "When this happens, our babies grow *flaco* . . . what? . . . skinny! Then they die."

Snakes drinking milk from mothers made as much sense to Tom as snakes using forks and knives. And about the mothers: Wouldn't they wake up?

Even so, Tom began to see dangers in every thin

shadow on the ground. And when branches moved above, the stirring of their leaves made their shadows underfoot seem even more like slithering snakes.

"And there are some spiders *y alacránes* . . . what do you say? Scorpions. And *pumas*. You know."

Tom didn't know. There were black widow spiders in Minnesota, but scorpions and pumas? Only on television—and only on educational shows he didn't watch anymore.

A thumping came from somewhere ahead and Ignacio turned to smile at Tom. *"Mi padre."*

Sure enough, in less than a minute, Tom saw Ignacio's father swinging a machete at some undergrowth around a waxy-leafed tree that was heavy with some kind of fruit.

"Hola," Ignacio called. His father lowered the machete and turned toward them.

Ignacio handed his father the basket of tortillas. The man took it to where a plastic milk bottle sat half filled with water. Tom saw that a thin layer of sand and mud had settled on the bottom of the bottle. Ignacio's father tipped the bottle to drink and the sand and mud swirled as the water disappeared into his mouth.

He and Ignacio spoke for a few moments, the

father talking even as he stuffed torn pieces of tortilla into his mouth. Ignacio nodded from time to time and Tom had the feeling they were discussing him. He wanted to know what they were saying.

Watching, Tom suddenly stopped ignoring the questions that had been trying to get his attention since the market. What did Senor Guerrero think of him, and of his sister? When would they be going back to find his parents? The thought of his parents made him catch his breath, almost hiccuping. Images of the market flashed through his mind and he closed his eyes to blot them out. But that sharpened them; he saw the man's legs twitching while blood poured from his neck. Tom's eyes flew open. He was relieved to find himself looking into Ignacio's eyes.

"*Mi papá* . . . he wants you to know that you are safe here . . . with us."

Tom nodded. "But I've been wondering . . ." He swallowed, feeling a little afraid of talking to Ignacio's father. He tried to smile. "The fighting . . . in Felicidad . . . what was that all about?" He glanced at Ignacio, hoping that the boy would translate for him.

Senor Guerrero spoke to Tom before his son had a chance. Tom strained to catch a Spanish word or two close enough to English that he could tell what the man was saying. When Ignacio's father stopped, Tom turned to the boy and pleaded with his eyes.

Ignacio frowned with the effort of trying to explain. "My father, he says that the soldiers from the government are not our friends. But the men, *los luchadores*, the . . . what do you say? The fighters are not our friends either. My father, he calls them *robolucionarios* . . . both . . ." Ignacio squinted, trying to think of the right word. His face brightened. "Both *robos*, robbers, and revolutionaries. The government in Mexico City and their soldiers take from us. And the *luchadores*, they will only do the same if they win."

"No good guys or bad guys?" Tom asked Ignacio.

Before Ignacio could answer, his father spoke. Intent, Tom turned to him.

When he stopped, Ignacio translated. "He says, they are both good and bad, together. One beats his burro in the name of *la gente* . . . the people. One beats his burro in the name of justice. But we . . . the people of the land . . . *los pobres* . . . we are the burros, and either way, we get beaten."

Tom didn't bother asking Ignacio. "You don't care who wins?" he asked Senor Guerrero.

The man frowned. He spoke and looked to his son to explain what he had said to Tom.

"Yes," Ignacio said. "He cares. The government is bad . . . corrupt . . . with many *ricos* . . . rich people who want only more. *Los robolucionarios,* they are from our villages and they are poor. If they win they will be better for a time. But then?" He shrugged. "They will forget and the beating . . . the oppression, it will start all over again."

"Will the soldiers come here?"

Ignacio's father replied, shaking his head.

"My father says the soldiers are afraid of these mountains. They believe we, the people who live here, are *locos* . . . crazy people with guns."

Ignacio's father smiled at these words and said, *"Es la verdad."*

Tom looked to Ignacio for help. "It is the truth, he says. Sometimes the people here can be crazy."

"But the fighting has stopped in Felicidad?"

Ignacio shook his head. "It is not safe. Maybe in two or three days."

"When can I let my parents know Philippa and I are all right?"

Ignacio shook his head again. "Maybe in a day or two. But for now"—he looked at his father, who nodded, and then back at Tom—"we must get the cows."

"Sure," Tom said. He turned to Senor Guerrero. "Thank you, sir."

Ignacio's father nodded, wiping sweat from his forehead.

"Follow me," Ignacio said.

As they walked toward the river, the thumping of the machete again filled the forest.

CHAPTER TEN

As Tom and Ignacio circled a tree dripping with avocados, Ignacio turned and smiled. "This tree has many testicles," he said.

Shocked, Tom wondered if he'd heard correctly.

Ignacio burst out laughing. "In the old language of my ancestors, the fruit of this tree is called that." He stepped closer and examined one. *"Ahuacatl,"* he said, picking it. He handed it to Tom.

Holding the avocado in his hand, Tom saw the truth in what Ignacio's ancestors had called it. He blushed, nodding. The shape and the texture of its skin was like that part of himself he'd never talked about with anybody. Tom imagined the tree festooned with jock straps, for protection as well as modesty. Or would that only call attention to what the jock straps would be holding?

He looked up from the fruit and laughed nervously, trying to imagine his grandmother comparing an avocado to something so personal. But why not? People today compared body parts to fruits and vegetables all the time. When was the last time he'd looked at a banana and seen only a banana?

"Who were your ancestors?" Tom asked.

Ignacio shrugged. *"Los indios,"* he said. *"Aztecas,* maybe. Who knows? *Mi abuela* knew, and my grandfather. But they are dead."

Ignacio took the avocado from Tom and cut it in two with his knife. He tossed the pit onto the ground and peeled away the skin, eating his half in two huge bites. Although Tom didn't especially like avocados, he took a nibble. It was surprisingly good. Almost sweet.

Tom finished the avocado as they walked along, side by side. His eyes flitted from the ground to the trees, following sounds as much as the colors of flowers and leaves. He was surprised when Ignacio made a little jump, plucking something from a tree.

Ignacio turned to Tom and held out his hand. He'd caught a long brown bug, its legs groping the air, feelers moving independently of each other. "You want?" Ignacio asked. "It is *jumile.*"

"No," Tom answered. He'd never been much of a bug person. And what would he do with a bug, anyway?

Ignacio popped the bug into his mouth. Tom gagged, watching Ignacio chew. "You eat them?"

"*Sí*. That kind of *insecto* is good." He flexed his arm muscle into a lump and smiled. "Makes a man *muy fuerte*."

"You're joking." Tom wondered if the avocado had gone to Ignacio's head.

"No." Ignacio looked puzzled. "Is true."

Ignacio may have been the one who'd swallowed the bug, but it was Tom's stomach that felt as if bugs were crawling around in it.

The ground was becoming sandier. The soil was loose, like the highest part of the beach where the waves couldn't reach, where walking was difficult. Suddenly, around a clump of bushes, he and Ignacio came to a river.

"*Río El Zapote*," Ignacio announced.

It wasn't much of a river, more like a creek. Ignacio walked up to it and bent over, scooping water into his cupped hands. Watching Ignacio drink, Tom realized how thirsty he was. The water sparkled from sunlight, but Tom had never drunk from a river before and had been warned against doing it many times. But if the water bad, Ignacio wouldn't be drinking it—would he? Tom hesitated.

When Ignacio splashed water onto his face and

around the back of his neck, Tom couldn't stand it any longer. He walked up to where Ignacio was and, cupping his hands, scooped water into his mouth. It wasn't warm, but not cool either, and it had a musky taste, reminding Tom of leaves and sand and mud. Even so, it felt good rushing down his throat.

"*Bueno. ¿Verdad?*" Ignacio asked. "The water, it comes from there." He pointed ahead, to where tall, spiky mountains seemed to have shredded a cloud that was drifting away from them, slipping behind the steep hill to their left.

They walked upstream. At first Tom avoided the water, not wanting to get his shoes wet. Ignacio, being barefooted, walked straight ahead, splashing with each step. When Tom finally landed a foot in the water, he gave up trying to keep dry. Tiny fish flashed, swimming away, as he, too, splashed along.

As they came around a bend in the river, Tom saw cattle ahead, maybe ten of them and a few calves, standing in water that barely covered their hooves. They were all looking at Tom and Ignacio, as if they'd been expecting them. Tom had never seen such sorry-looking cows. Their bony hips looked like tents collapsing around a crumpled frame of poles. Their eyes were dull and stupid. They made standing look exhausting.

One of the cows had a dangling cactus pad stuck to her lower lip. The sand where they stood was trampled, pocked with hoof prints, the separate streams bleary. The closer he got to the cattle, the more cow flops Tom noticed.

The water he'd drunk had come from this. He might as well have scooped water from a toilet.

"These yours?" he asked.

"*Sí,*" Ignacio said.

The cattle hardly seemed to notice as Tom and Ignacio walked around them. Making war cries, Ignacio clapped his hands and threw rocks to get their attention. Mooing, the cows began to move slowly, as if the sand gave them no traction. Without warning, they made a sharp turn to the right.

Ignacio trotted in that direction and, waving his hands, got them to straighten out only to have them turn to the left. Tom joined in.

"They always like this?" he called out to Ignacio.

Ignacio laughed. "Yes," he said. "But look." He barked and growled like a dog, rushing the cows, dodging back and forth. The cows sprang forward and fell into a straight line. Tom began to bark and growl, too. A cow wheeled around and lowered her head, swinging it in Tom's direction. Her calf seemed stuck to her side. Tom froze.

Gone was the dull, stupid look. It seemed to Tom that the cow wanted to make hamburger out of him.

Before Tom could cry out for help, Ignacio jumped in front of the cow and whacked it on the face with his fist. The dull thud made Tom think that the cow's head might be hollow. Boggling in fear, the cow seemed to fold up sideways like an empty paper towel tube. As she ran to catch up with the others, she lifted her tail, splattering watery manure into both sand and river, almost hitting her calf.

"Thanks!" Tom gasped.

"*De nada,*" Ignacio said.

"What was she going to do?"

Ignacio smiled. "Maybe she loves you."

Tom made a face, and then, unexpectedly, a laugh bubbled up from his gut. "Sure," he said, smiling back.

The cattle moved incredibly slowly and Tom found himself needing to visit a bathroom. He was exhausted from trying to push the cattle along while pressing his butt cheeks together when they caught sight of the thatched roofs of the Guerreros's ranch. He was splattered with cow flops and his shoes were soaked. His socks had slipped into balls under his arches and he hadn't been able to stop and fix them. Chasing a calf, he'd run through a patch of something that stung his arms. At the time, he'd hoped the pain would soon subside, like that from stinging nettles. Instead, the stinging had turned to splotches, pink-yellow—as nasty looking as poison ivy. Damn! he thought. It's going to wreck my tan.

At least now the cows seemed to know where to go. Bawling in their excitement, they formed a raggedy single line and headed for a fence of cactus near the corral where Ignacio kept his horse.

"Hey! Tom!"

Philippa ran up to him, wisps of hair sticking to the sweat on her face. She was followed by two of the smaller kids, one of them the naked boy. "Hi, Filly," Tom said, grinning at her. "What've you been doing?"

"Guess what?" she asked breathlessly. "I got *nine eggs*! Nine! They were everywhere. Even in that place there"—she pointed to a hut—"where everybody sleeps. And look!" She held out her arm. "One of the chickens pecked me!"

Tom saw a round bruise on her forearm, faint green around the edge with a button of dried blood in the middle. And instead of being hysterical about it, she was excited! "You okay?" he asked. At home she would cry for a Band-Aid at the slightest scratch.

"Sure!" she said. "And I'm teaching these kids English!" She turned to the naked boy. "Say 'Princess Philippa,'" she ordered him.

Smiling up at her, the boy said, "Pin-sass Pill-ee-paw."

Philippa squealed with pleasure. "See!" she said, turning back to Tom. "I'll show you something neat."

"Sure, but . . ." She grabbed his hand and started dragging him around the cooking hut before he could ask her where the bathroom was. The boy and the girl followed.

Tom saw several chickens strutting and pecking. Around them, like little yellow dust balls, ran six or seven chicks.

"Look at where these little ones go." Philippa pulled him over to a tube of wire fencing that stood on end. Inside was an old chipped plate piled with cracked corn. Chicks ran in and out of the holes in the fencing.

"See?" Philippa said. "The little ones can eat without the bigger ones, or the pigs, getting their food!"

"Neat," Tom said, through clenched teeth. He lowered his voice. "Do you know where the bathroom is?"

Philippa shrugged. "Nope," she said. "Come on, Edgardo," she said to the boy, "and Katarina," she said to a girl, who had her hands clasped behind her back.

The three of them ran around the cooking hut. Deliberately, Tom made his way to the courtyard. Ignacio was shutting the corral gate on the cattle. "Hey, Ignacio. Where's the bathroom?"

Ignacio pointed to a little building standing by itself and no wider or taller than a door. "See you in *la cocina* . . . you know . . ." He pointed to the shed with the pepper roof.

Tom nodded. He was beginning to understand: *La cocina* was the kitchen.

He walked toward the outhouse. He'd used chemical toilets before, and he hoped that this outhouse didn't stink like them or splash blue-green solution on his bottom while he sat.

He hadn't taken more than a couple of steps, when a pig ran up to him. He was tempted to pat its head, as if it were a dog. Before he could do that, another pig trotted over to join them. Spooked, Tom kept walking.

Searching for the door, he walked around to the other side of the outhouse. There was no door, so he was glad the opening faced away from the huts Ignacio called home.

The outhouse smelled much better than he thought it would. Maybe not having a door kept it aired out. He dropped his jeans and sat gingerly, not wanting to get splinters from the rough-looking wood.

He tensed, hearing a low rumbling sound that was not coming from him. And then, from below, came a snarl and a squeal. When the noises grew louder, Tom stood quickly and turned to face the hole. Animals?

He saw movement. The snarling grew quiet, becoming low, nervous grunts. In the dim light, he made out a pig's snout. And then another. How had the pigs gotten down there?

"Shoo!" he yelled down the hole, banging on the board with his fist. The pigs squealed and disappeared. Tom waited a few moments and, when they didn't show their snouts again, climbed onto the board and perched.

As he steadied himself, he heard renewed grunting from below.

Serve them right if they get hit, he thought. "Bombs away," he muttered, thinking of coconuts.

The grunting again turned to squealing. Tom sprang from the board and pulled up his jeans without bothering to look for anything to wipe with. Holding his breath, he peered again into the hole.

They were fighting! The pigs were fighting to eat his shit!

No wonder the outhouse smelled so good.

Zipping and buttoning as he hurried away, Tom promised himself that he'd never again eat even a tiny bite of bacon for the rest of his life.

CHAPTER ELEVEN

Tom sat with Ignacio against the front wall of the cooking hut. Watching the other kids playing helped keep his mind off the rash on his arms, which was worse now. But the way the kids ran around reminded him of the people in the market, trying to escape gunfire and soldiers and *robolucionarios*. These throbbing images were like a rash in his mind. He was grateful that Philippa hadn't seen the man getting shot in the neck. He wondered about his parents. How frantic they must be about Philippa! Maybe even about him. Had they risked danger, trying to find the two of them? Were they hurt? Suddenly the man on the floor had his father's face, and the twitching legs wore his father's sandals.

He groaned, bowing his head and shaking it, trying to scatter these thoughts like flies. He was left feeling as bare and exposed as the fish guts he'd seen on the beach.

Ignacio laughed and Tom looked up at Philippa, Katarina, Edgardo, and the older boy, who were each dragging plastic soda bottles filled with dirt around a post in the center of the courtyard. Below their lids, each bottle was tied to a long leash made of short bits of string knotted together.

The four of them ran in loopy circles, trying to keep their strings untangled, their bottles from being hit by the others, and—he could hardly believe it—laughing when they stumbled or fell.

Philippa was having a great time, yelling and shrieking louder than anybody else until her bottle was kicked by the older boy. His bare foot cracked the plastic. Dirt poured from its wound. Philippa skidded to a stop and stared as if it were bleeding, and then looked up to the boy who was still laughing and now running toward Edgardo, whose naked butt seemed to have a hard time keeping up with the rest of him as he darted first one way and then the other.

"Livorio!" she shouted, stamping her feet in anger. "Look what you did!"

Livorio stopped and twisted around to look at her, his arms loose and his shoulders rising and falling with panting. He smiled, but looked puzzled by her anger.

"You wrecked it!" Philippa cried. Tom could hear tears in her voice. He knew what would come next: The Tantrum. "How can I play with a broken bottle?" Her whine was beginning to sound like the whistle of an approaching train.

Edgardo giggled and ran up to Philippa's bottle, flipping it over with his foot. When his bottle skidded in front of Katarina, she kicked it so hard that it jumped Livorio's string.

They hadn't understood Philippa at all, Tom realized, as they began laughing and playing again. To his surprise, Philippa closed her mouth and squared her shoulders. She swallowed her disappointment and, with great effort, walked back into the game. Soon she was laughing and shrieking and running, her bottle obeying each little jerk of her string better now than when it had been filled with dirt.

"Your sister, she runs well," Ignacio said.

Tom hesitated before he nodded. The other kids seemed much more agile. He suspected that they were being careful not to frustrate Philippa too much.

"When I see her, I think of my sister who died last year," Ignacio added.

"You had a sister who died?" Tom didn't know anybody back home whose sister or brother had died. He'd sometimes wished that Philippa would die, that he'd be an only child again, but only because it was a safe wish. It would never happen.

"*Sí,*" Ignacio said. "She laughed all the time. And she liked to win."

"I . . . I'm sorry," Tom said.

Ignacio shrugged but sounded sad. "*Es la vida.* Life." He touched Tom's arm with a finger. "When did this happen?"

It was then that Tom realized he'd been scratching. He looked at the skin that had balled up under his fingernails. A tear of pus slid down his arm and dropped to the ground.

"This afternoon. Getting the cattle." He lifted his arm for Ignacio to examine. "Is there anything I can do about it?"

Ignacio nodded. "In *la cocina.*"

The kitchen was even hotter than before. Whatever was bubbling away in the large pot smelled even better now. Ignacio's mother was grinding mushy whole corn on a flat rock by holding a matching loaf-shaped rock in both hands. Tom wondered if she ever left this hut. She nodded as Ignacio explained what he wanted.

Ignacio walked to some shelves on one side of the hut and pulled off a clear glass bottle. Ignacio extracted the cork with his back teeth. He held the bottle to Tom's nose.

Tom sneezed. The fumes from it were stronger than fumes from a gas pump, a combination of turpentine and the whiskey his father drank sometimes. "What is it?" he asked.

Ignacio took the cork from his mouth. "Mescal," he said. "La Esperanza is *muy famosa* . . . famous for its mescal." Lifting the bottle to his lips, he took a sip, made a face, and shuddered. "*¡Como un burro!*" he gasped, holding it out to Tom.

Just lifting the bottle to his mouth made Tom's eyes water. Plugging the opening with his tongue, he let a trickle of the mescal seep into his throat. It might as well have been gasoline. He quickly lowered the bottle and uncorked his tongue, which felt as if it had fallen asleep. "Wow!" he wheezed. The taste of the liquor was different from its smell—reminding him of the time he'd missed his armpit and sprayed deodorant into his face instead. His voice seemed as shocked by the mescal as his mouth. It was strong stuff and he looked at his arms, hoping to see instant improvement. "Should I drink some more?" he managed to ask in a whisper.

"No, no, no," Ignacio chuckled. He took a handful of the hem of Tom's polo shirt and let a glug of mescal seep into the cloth. He dabbed at Tom's fore-arm.

It stung. Like red ants biting. Tom was about to jerk his arm away, but, as quickly as it started, the stinging began to fade. Where Ignacio had moistened his arms, the skin was now as numb as his tongue had been.

"Mescal," Ignacio said, pouring a little more onto Tom's shirt and going over a few spots again. "Good medicine. For *la cabeza*"—he pointed to his head—"*y por todo el cuerpo.*" He gestured down his body. "*Medicina más buena por todo.*"

Maybe it was that slug of mescal, but Tom thought he understood, and smiled.

Once Ignacio had doctored both arms, Ignacio's mother, who had continued grinding the soft corn, spoke to her son. He nodded and fetched a basket near the shelves where he had returned the bottle.

He handed the basket to Tom. "We must get some things for eating."

Tom was grateful for the fresh air outside. It felt good on the skin of his arms.

Tom heard laughter coming from the corral where the cattle had been penned. He and Ignacio walked past it, into the forest. The farther they got from the huts, the denser the undergrowth became.

Ignacio began picking green leaves here and there and handing them to Tom to put into the basket. Everything Ignacio picked looked like really ugly weeds to Tom, but then this was a different kind of supermarket from what he was used to. It seemed that the land around was the Guerrero family's store—for fruit and greens and meat. Even bugs. Tom's stomach rumbled. He wondered what they would be having for dinner. Whatever was bubbling in the big pot in *la cocina*, he hoped.

"*La última,*" Ignacio finally said, when the basket was full. He took the basket from Tom as they walked back to the huts. Ignacio seemed lost in his own thoughts, and so was Tom. Tom couldn't stop thinking about his parents. He found himself wishing that they were here—that they could meet Ignacio's parents and see how well Philippa was doing with Ignacio's brothers and sister. And how well he was doing with all the new stuff here—avocados and outhouse pigs and the horse and herding cattle. He hoped they would be proud.

Philippa ran to meet them.

"I got to help feed the chickens!" she said, jumping up and down. "And now we're feeding the horse. And the cows, too! Want to help?"

"I guess," Tom said, feeling low in energy but

letting Philippa pull him along toward the cactus corral.

Inside, Ignacio's father was dividing up a large pile of tangled brush that looked like the stuff he'd been cutting with his machete. Tom understood now what he'd been doing in the papaya grove—cutting food for the horse and cattle.

Philippa ran to him and tugged at the man's shirttail.

He turned and smiled. Piling brush into her arms, he pointed to a corner of the corral. Tom approached and held out his arms. After he was loaded up, Ignacio's father waved his hands, motioning him to take his armload to the cattle.

Tom dropped more than half of it along the way. And the leaves irritated the rash on his arms. He delivered what was left to the middle of the corral, careful not to get too close to the cattle, who were bunched together in one corner. They stood still for a moment, staring at him, looking suspicious.

Shadows were lengthening as he walked back for the rest of the brush and then toward the cooking hut. Tom felt chilled for the first time since coming to Mexico—except for his few attempts to bond with the ocean. The goose bumps stung where they puckered his rash. He studied his forearm. It looked about the same, and he decided it would need another dose of mescal after dinner.

Yellow light from the doorway fell onto the ground, flickering like a patch of oily water. The sound of voices came out in waves. He ducked his head to go inside.

Ignacio's father was already sitting at the small table that had been pulled from one wall. A plate sat on the table, a napkin covering what it held. A stack of tortillas, no doubt.

Over the table hung a lantern. There was only one other chair, close to the fire, and it was empty. Everyone else stood around in the fringes of the lantern's light while Ignacio's mother busied herself at the bubbling pot. The smell coming from it fogged the air, and once more Tom's stomach rumbled.

Ignacio's father gestured toward the empty chair. "*Siéntate,*" he said to Tom.

Tom found Ignacio's eyes and questioned him with his own. Ignacio nodded toward the chair.

As Tom walked toward the chair, he passed the pot and peeked into it.

He felt his stomach sink into his intestines. Nodding and bouncing on top of a bubbling broth was a head. A pig's head. With eyelids partway open. Its pig nose was crinkled, as if sniffing. It might have been the pig head he'd seen in the market, only smaller.

Tom couldn't hide the horror in his face as he looked at Ignacio. "It is *pozole,*" Ignacio said, gently. "*Muy sabroso,*" he added. "You will like it."

Tom took his seat of honor and looked across to Ignacio's father. "*Bienvenida,* Tom," said Senor Guerrero. He smiled, showing two gold teeth.

Tom tried smiling back. He noticed Philippa, standing behind Senor Guerrero and next to Edgardo. She looked tired, as if she were almost asleep on her feet. He didn't know if it was allowed or not, but he took a chance, beckoning to her with a nod of his head.

She came and climbed into his lap, curling up, resting her head against his chest. "I miss Mom and Dad," she whispered.

Tom nuzzled his chin into her hair. "I do, too. But they're all right. And so are we." Ignacio's mother placed a steaming blue enamel bowl in front of him, upon which puddles of grease moved as if they were alive. "We'll see Mom and Dad soon," he added, watching Senor Guerrero scoop the stew to his mouth with a piece he'd torn off a tortilla and folded partway over.

Tom was no longer hungry, but, working around

his now sleeping sister, he reached for a tortilla, ripped a piece off, and dipped it into the bowl. He quickly popped it into his mouth.

It was smooth as gravy but souplike. The taste woke the hunger that had been curled up and asleep in his gut. He reached again and scooped out more.

CHAPTER TWELVE

Tom felt a poke in his ribs and the weight of a hand on his shoulder.

"Lay off!" he mumbled, and gripped his blanket tighter, pulling it closer to his chin.

He felt another poke.

"Come on!" he groaned, staying on his back but turning his head away from the poked shoulder.

It felt too early to be wakened. Waves of snoring had broken over him all night, constant as the sea. Wind and varmints scurrying through the thatch of the roof were more distracting than a ceiling fan. It had taken Tom a long time to fall asleep.

It hadn't helped that he'd slept on a mat with Livorio curled up on one side and Philippa burrowing into him on the other. He didn't know which one of them had the sharpest elbows and knees. Except for Edgardo, who'd slept with his mother and father on their mattress across the room, all the kids had shared this mat—Katarina against the wall on Philippa's other side and Ignacio on the far edge.

The family had settled in to sleep quickly, lying down in their clothes. They'd pushed up against each other. Tom had enjoyed the closeness for a while— the night air had been chilly, the blankets thin. After Livorio draped an arm over Tom's chest and sighed, breathing softly into Tom's shirt, Tom had felt the boy heat up like an electric blanket.

Just as Tom had been about to fall asleep, he'd heard snorting. A pig had wandered into the hut and was sniffing and rooting around their feet. Ignacio had kicked out, pulling the blanket off everybody, sending the pig squealing from the hut.

And there had been yipping and barking from out in the forest—like a dog trying to sing opera. Coyotes or wild dogs?

And all night long his arms had itched. He'd almost gone crazy trying not to scratch them.

Tom felt yet another poke. He gritted his teeth in anger, turned his head to face the ceiling, and opened his eyes a crack to the watery light. He listened for the sounds of other people breathing. He heard nothing, which jolted him awake. His eyes caught movement to his left and he looked to see a chicken

standing on his shoulder. The chicken's head twitched
and aimed a single beady eye at him. Swinging ham-
merlike, it pecked the blanket over his chest.

"Hey!" He sat up and the chicken seemed to explode. Feathers churning, more cloud than bird, it
flew toward the door. He saw, on a corner of the
blanket, an egg. He'd almost rolled into it. What
kind of stupid chicken would lay eggs on a bed while
somebody was sleeping in it?

Tom staggered to his feet and looked around. He
was the last one up. Children's voices came from
outside. He stretched. His clothes felt stiff with dirt.
His arms looked better. Even though the scent of
mescal had faded, Tom caught a whiff of it coming
from his arms and shirt. He combed his fingers
through his hair and sniffed his armpits. Between
them and the mescal, he smelled as if he'd spent the
night in a Dumpster behind a liquor store.

How did Ignacio and his family manage to look
so neat and clean all the time?

Bending over, he picked up the egg. He liked the
way it felt in the palm of his hand, smooth and
warm.

His stomach rumbled as he stepped outside, but
he didn't feel hungry. In fact, the thought of food

made him queasy. Too much of the food in Mexico came with eyes that stared at him while he ate.

The sky was the blue of tissue paper, the thin clouds looking like crinkles. Little red birds flashed from branch to branch in the lime tree next to the cooking hut. A lounging pig hoisted itself to its feet and trotted toward him, the corners of its mouth curled up in a pig smile. It rubbed up against his leg like a cat, feeling smooth, almost slippery. Tom reached down to pat it. Stroking from back to front, the pig was as prickly as the bristles of a toothbrush.

He crossed the courtyard to the cooking hut, stepped inside, and, through the smoky air, saw everyone gathered around the hearth while Senora Guerrero made tortillas. She smiled up at him. *"¿Tienes hambre?"* she asked. Her voice was gentle and low. Before he could answer, she plucked a tortilla from the griddle and held it out to him. He handed her the egg as he took the tortilla. Her smile grew. *"Gracias,"* she said.

"Where'd you find it?" Philippa asked, skipping over to him. She hugged his waist, pressing her ear against him as if she were listening to his belly button.

Tom was afraid she would think it was weird that a chicken had practically laid an egg on him while he slept. "Around," he said, rubbing the top of her head with his fingertips.

"Guess what?" she said, pushing away from him. "The momma is going to wash clothes! And we're going to help!"

Tom glanced at Ignacio, who grinned at him. "Is true," Ignacio said. "Come. We must prepare."

Propped up outside the doorway was a large zinc tub with handles. Beside the tub was a bucket. Ignacio motioned for Tom to help him flip the tub over and carry it to the courtyard. A few minutes later, Ignacio's mother came from the cooking hut, clutching a bundle of clothes tied together with string. She lifted the bundle onto her head, balanced it with one hand, and marched across the courtyard in the direction of the river.

Before Tom and Ignacio could lift the tub, Edgardo climbed into it and put the bucket on his head like a helmet. Laughing, Tom and Ignacio hoisted the tub and followed Ignacio's mother. The other children skipped around each other and the dog, who barked and danced on his hind legs. A pig lifted its head to see what was going on and then let it drop with a thud to continue its nap.

Edgardo did everything he could to make holding the tub difficult. He rocked back and forth and twice grabbed the front edge, leaning forward so far that the bucket fell off his head onto the ground. Each time, Ignacio picked it up by hooking the handle with his foot. When Edgardo began kicking the bottom of the tub with his heels, Ignacio looked over to Tom and nodded. *"Uno, dos, tres,"* he said, tipping the tub forward.

Edgardo tumbled out with a cry, landing on his back. It must have hurt, Tom thought, and for a moment Edgardo looked as if he was going to cry. But as he looked up at Ignacio and Tom, his face hardened. Sticking out his tongue, he raced to catch up with the other kids, leaving the bucket for them.

"What is it like in *el norte?"* Ignacio asked once they'd fallen into an easy rhythm without Edgardo squirming in the tub.

Tom didn't know where to start. It was straight lines and clean clothes. It was cool, clean water coming from faucets, ready to drink. It was thick grass where grass should be and sidewalks for walking and cars whispering as they went by. It was . . .

"Are people rich . . . in *el norte?"* Ignacio pressed.

Tom had never thought of his family as rich—there were so many families who had more money than his. But he found himself nodding. "Yes," he said, thinking of Ignacio's family's truck and the huts they lived in. Even the simplest things at home, like the old, scorched toaster on the counter next to the refrigerator, seemed rich compared with cooking tortillas over a wood fire, on a griddle made of a sheet of wavy metal.

"How do you pass time?" Ignacio asked.

Once again, so many answers sprang into his head, he found it difficult to say anything. Surf the Web? How could he explain about computers to Ignacio? "Mostly," he said, "I go to the mall with my best buddy, Henderson, and hang out."

"Mall?" Ignacio frowned. "Why do you go if it is bad?"

Tom didn't understand. "The mall isn't bad. It's great!"

Ignacio shook his head. *"En español, 'mal' is una palabra . . .* um, a word . . . meaning 'bad.'"

Tom was about to argue, when he understood. He smiled. "My parents think it's bad. The mall, I mean. But in English, 'mall' is . . . it's like a market. Like where your dad sells masks. Only really, *really* big. And fancy."

"Do you sell things at your mall?"

"No. We hang around, my buddies and me. Sometimes Henderson and I go to Pretzel City and we say nice things to Sandra, if she's working there, so she'll give us free pretzels." Anticipating Ignacio's question, he tried to explain. "A pretzel is like round bread . . . more like a bread rope, all tied up, kind of . . . with salt on it."

Ignacio nodded. "You like this Sandra?"

"No! She's a dog! We only pretend, so she'll give us pretzels." Geez, Tom thought. I sound like a creep. "They throw the pretzels out if they don't get sold after a while anyway. We're really doing her . . . them . . . a favor." He still sounded like a creep.

Ignacio shook his head, as if to say he didn't understand.

"You should come to visit us some time," Tom said.

"Yes?"

"There's so much, where I live. It makes me feel stupid trying to describe it."

Ignacio nodded. "Yes," he said, as if agreeing that Tom sounded stupid.

They were within sight of the river, and Tom saw Philippa splashing in some shallow water with Katarina and Edgardo. Livorio was helping his mother lift the bundle from her head.

Tom and Ignacio walked up to her. She pointed to a place in the river where she wanted the tub. While Ignacio and Tom took turns filling it, Ignacio's mother reached for Edgardo and sat him in an eddy. She began scrubbing him, and Katarina and Philippa ran upriver, shrieking.

"Here," Ignacio said, handing the bucket to Tom. He and Ignacio ran after them. Ignacio caught Philippa. Livorio caught Katarina, and, by the time the girls had been dragged back to be washed, Tom had filled the tub. Senora Guerrero gave both girls a quick scrubbing under their clothes and rinsed out their hair. Philippa laughed the whole time, especially when Senora Guerrero tickled her ribs.

The children washed, Senora Guerrero untied the bundle and took out a shirt, which she rubbed with a huge bar of yellow soap, then beat against a rock. She rinsed the shirt in the river and finally dropped it into the tub of water.

"Livorio," Ignacio called, beckoning his brother with his arm. Ignacio turned to Tom. "We must wash ourselves . . . *los hombres.*"

Ignacio's mother looked up from her washing and spoke. He nodded and answered Tom's questioning look by saying, "When we are finished, my mother wants us to take the wet clothes back, and to hang them to . . . to dry."

They walked up the river, and when Katarina, Philippa, and Edgardo tried to follow, Ignacio spoke to Katarina in Spanish. Sticking out her tongue, she spun around and ran back toward their mother. Katarina called to them and Philippa and Edgardo followed.

The boys were quiet. Tom didn't know how much English Livorio knew, and didn't want him to feel left out if he talked with Ignacio. Besides, it felt good to be quiet, not to have to think about anything for a while.

Around the first bend, they turned from the river toward a large clump of trees. Tom saw a stream flowing from them; for a time its water was a clear, wavy ribbon within the murkier water of the river. Ignacio plunged through the trees, followed by his brother. Tom batted at leafy branches, trying to stay close.

They entered a side canyon, narrow at first, but soon opening up. Ahead, Tom heard a hiss, as if somebody had left the water running in the bathroom sink back home. When they rounded a short rock outcropping, he saw a waterfall tumbling down a cliff. At the bottom, water skidded over a rock that jutted out, making rainbow colors as it fell into a little pool.

Mist beaded Tom's eyelashes. He blinked it away to see Ignacio and Livorio walk into the pool. They peeled off their shirts and waded until they stood in the falling water. Tom pulled off his shirt and followed.

The water was freezing and he sucked in his breath. It splatted on top of his head and ran like a hundred snakes slithering down his spine. His jeans grew so heavy with water that they began to slip off his hips. He yanked them up, wishing he was wearing underpants for once.

Ignacio and his brother set to work washing themselves. They rubbed their hair, as if lathering it, moving down to their necks and faces. Tom did the same. It was crowded under the waterfall, and his elbows clashed with both Ignacio's and Livorio's as he scrubbed at his hair and then under his arms. Tipping his head up, he let water pour into his mouth and spill over his face and chin.

It was then his jeans finally let go, plopping into the water, settling around his feet.

Almost choking, Tom snapped his head forward and grabbed for the jeans, but too late. Both Ignacio and Livorio looked as surprised as he. Without a word, they turned from his nakedness and continued washing themselves.

Tom turned his back to them. For people who let their little brother run around naked, Tom thought they were being strangely prudish. He pulled up his jeans and continued scrubbing with one hand.

When Tom turned around again, he saw Ignacio step from the waterfall and shake himself like a dog. Water flew from his head and shoulders.

Tom followed. "Hey, Ignacio!" he called, bending over and scooping with his hands. When Ignacio turned to him, Tom heaved water onto him.

Sputtering, Ignacio's eyes widened. When Livorio staggered over to his brother, Tom was ready, filling the boy's mouth with water when he opened it to speak.

Water soon filled the air. Tom grabbed his jeans as they began sliding off, and laughed. With his free arm he tackled Ignacio, who fell into Livorio, toppling him.

CHAPTER THIRTEEN

The tub of wet, clean clothes was almost as heavy as when Edgardo had been sitting in it. The three of them took turns at the two handles as they silently trudged away from the river. Tom was grateful that his wet clothes kept him cool.

Back home, if he'd been walking with Henderson for this long in silence, he'd have felt something was wrong. The squishing of his wet shoes seemed especially loud without conversation. Tom glanced at the two brothers often, but Ignacio and Livorio didn't seem uncomfortable. Tom tried to relax and, to distract himself, began looking around. For the first time, he was able to see where the cattle had been herded, ripping small branches off trees as they went, even taking bites from paddle-shaped cactuses. There were big-leafed plants and spindly trees that Dr. Seuss might have invented and then rejected, thinking they were too weird.

Even with all the strange, interesting things to look at, Tom was glad to see thatched roofs ahead. As they walked toward the cooking hut, Tom noticed a steer tied to the post in the courtyard. It looked as dejected as somebody eating alone in the school cafeteria. It shied from them as they passed, lifting its tail as if to poop. Nothing came out.

Before he could ask Ignacio why the steer was there, Philippa ran from the hut, crying. Tom staggered, trying to keep hold of the tub, as she threw herself onto him.

"What's wrong, Filly?" he asked, letting Livorio take the handle from him. He patted her head, not knowing what else to do, watching Ignacio and Livorio totter to the cooking shed, where they dropped the tub and plopped down next to it.

"We . . . *caught* . . . it," she managed to say. "We caught the chicken, just like the mother told us to. But"—she looked up at him, her face streaked with tears—"I didn't know she was going to kill it!" Her sorrow flashed to anger, and she pushed away from him, glaring as if it were his fault. "She just grabbed it by the legs and *stabbed* it in the neck and *killed* it!"

She came back to him and buried her face again in his still-wet shirt, sobbing.

Tom stroked her shoulder. "You don't have to eat it, you know."

He meant his words to be comforting. But she pushed away from him again.

"Not eat it?" she shouted. "*Not* eat it? After it died for us?" She stamped her foot. The old Philippa. It was comforting—and irritating. "We *have* to eat it! We can't just let it die for nothing! Don't you understand *anything*?"

For a moment, he felt as if he didn't. He watched as she disappeared into the cooking hut.

"*Pues,*" Ignacio said, heaving himself onto his feet. "We must hang these for *mi mamá.*" He walked toward two trees with a rope strung between them, leaving Tom and Livorio to bring the tub. Tom watched as each boy took a shirt and draped it over the rope, smoothing out the wrinkles. He began to do the same.

When the clothes were hung and making small puddles in the dirt below, Ignacio turned to Tom and smiled. "Want to play some *fútbol* . . . how do you call it? Ah! . . . soccer?"

Tom nodded and Ignacio ran off, coming back with a ball—probably the same one that had hit him in the face.

Ignacio was a good teacher, and soon he and Tom

were passing the ball back and forth, even between the steer's legs. The steer didn't seem to notice.

The playing stopped when Tom accidentally kicked the ball into the cooking hut. They heard Ignacio's mother's cry, "Ai-e-e-e!"

But before either of them could get to the hut to retrieve the ball and collect whatever scolding they had coming to them, Ignacio jerked his head over his shoulder.

"Truck," he said. "Coming here. We must get *mi papi.*" He yelled something to his mother and trotted off toward the forest. Tom followed. The growl of an approaching vehicle was drowned out by barking as the dog became excited.

Steady thumping led them to Ignacio's father. Panting, Ignacio spoke, Spanish words fluttering from his mouth. Grunting, Senor Guerrero tucked his machete under his arm and, scraping the sweat from his face with the edge of his hand, began walking quickly toward the settlement.

Ignacio and Tom followed close enough behind that Tom could smell the sourness of sweat from Senor Guerrero's clothes. When they got to the sleeping hut, Ignacio held Tom back, letting his father enter the courtyard alone.

From where they stood in the shade of the hut,

Tom and Ignacio saw a yellow sedan, old but not too old, parked next to the Guerreros's truck. Three men were gathered around its hood, all of them facing Ignacio's father. They were speaking to him, sometimes all at once, and he occasionally nodded, but said nothing.

"Who are these men?" Tom asked. The other children were clustered behind their father, Philippa's head glowing against a field of black hair.

"Some men from La Esperanza," Ignacio muttered. "¡Cabrón!"

Tom looked at Ignacio. He had the feeling they weren't just any men from La Esperanza, but something about the way Ignacio was staring at them made him feel he shouldn't ask more about who they were. "What are they talking about?"

"You and your sister."

Tom pictured the faces of the people in La Esperanza as they looked when Senor Guerrero had driven through the town. He'd wondered what they'd been thinking. "What about us?"

"They want to know why you are here."

When Senor Guerrero spoke, his voice was calm and firm.

"What is he saying?" Tom asked, noticing that one of the men was staring at him. Tom stepped back farther into the shadows.

"He is telling these men how we saved you in the market . . . when the shooting started."

The men listened and then spoke among themselves for a few moments. Their leader, a man with a hat like a cowboy's, but smaller, looked at Senor Guerrero and spoke a few words. But Ignacio's father cut him off with a wave of his hand. He sounded angry. The man with the hat shrugged and spoke again. The other men nodded.

"What's going on?" Tom whispered.

Ignacio replied rapidly, trying to keep up with what the men were saying. "Those men, they are asking my father to give you to them. So they can get money for you. They say they will give some of the money to my father, but they will use what they get to buy guns for when the government soldiers come. They tell my father that we can use the money to help the people against *los robos* in our government. 'We will not hurt them,' they say. 'And those rich *Americanos* . . . what is a few thousand *dólares* to them?' But my father says no. That he will take you back to your parents. That he will not ask for money . . . even for buying guns to defend ourselves. He says asking money for children, it is worse than begging. That he is an honest man, a man of principle."

"They want our parents to pay money for us? That stinks!" Tom blurted. He said it loud enough that the three men from La Esperanza looked over to him.

"*Sí,*" said Ignacio, motioning for Tom to be quiet.

The leader turned back to Ignacio's father and spoke again. Senor Guerrero stiffened. The color in his face deepened. He yelled at the men, shaking his fist in their faces.

"Why is he angry?" Tom asked.

"Because they say my father is always thinking that he's better than everybody else. They say my father will help them ... give you and your sister to them ... or they wouldn't be surprised if our ranch, it might catch on fire and our animals might be killed."

Tom was shocked. "What did your father say?"

Ignacio looked grim. "He is telling these men to leave and never come back. He is telling them that men can fight for *la justicia* without hiding behind children, without risking the lives of children."

The leader silenced Ignacio's father by slamming his fist onto the hood of the car. He said several words through clenched teeth and then turned, glaring at the shadows by the hut where Tom watched.

Slowly the men got into the old sedan, started the engine, and made a wide circle around the courtyard before leaving. The steer stared, its eyes white with fear, as they went by.

Ignacio's mother came from the cooking hut, wiping her hands on a piece of cloth stained with blood. She walked up to her husband and spoke to him quietly. He nodded and followed her into the hut, his shoulders sagging. The children stood where they were, silent, with worried faces.

Tom took a deep breath. "What will your father do?" he asked.

"I do not know," Ignacio answered.

"And who is this man, anyway?"

Ignacio didn't answer.

Before he could ask again, Tom was next to Philippa. He reached out a hand to her, and she took it. He pulled her close, holding her head to his stomach, covering her ears as he rocked her back and forth. "What would happen if Philippa and I went with those men? Would they hurt us?"

Ignacio looked to the pepper-covered roof of the cooking hut. "No," he said. "They would not hurt a child. But, like me, you are almost a man. They might hurt you. Maybe . . . a little. Until your parents pay."

CHAPTER FOURTEEN

The steer tied to the post began bellowing that night. Tom counted between bellows—one Mississippi, two Mississippi. Every six seconds, the steer cried out, starting low, with an upward curl at the end. It was a hollow sound, echoing inside the steer's mouth before being swallowed.

Nobody else seemed bothered. The snoring in the hut was as loud as the night before. Every so often, a fart wafted through the hut, smelling of chicken.

The dinner had been good. Tom had eaten more than he had for days. Ignacio's mother had ground up some of the red peppers and added their powder to the chicken. The pepper had been hot in his mouth at first, but then warmed his stomach, soothing it. It warmed his stomach still.

Livorio's legs twitched and Tom rolled carefully onto his back, not wanting to disturb Philippa. It was still strange trying to sleep in a room with so many people, but several times he'd almost dozed off. Each time the steer had bellowed, and he was startled awake. The mournful sound made his chest ache with loneliness. It made him long for his parents, long to know if they were thinking of him, and Philippa. Each bellow pushed him closer to tears, making him want to know if their chests were aching as much as his.

When he could stand it no longer, he slipped from under the blanket and crawled to the doorway. He crept into silvery night light that made the pocked dirt of the courtyard look like a moonscape. He squatted and looked toward the steer.

It had wound its rope around the post. The rope curled down, peppermint-candy style, pulling the steer's head to the ground. It tugged at the post, which tightened the rope further, making it impossible to lift its snot-slimed nose more than a few inches above the ground.

Maybe, he thought, he could help the animal. He stood and padded across the moonlit courtyard. The steer swallowed its next bellow. Moon-glazed eyes strained to look at him as he approached.

"That's okay," Tom said, keeping his voice quiet and calm. He reached for the steer's head but it pulled away from him, grinding its nose into the post. "I'm trying to help!" Tom whispered. He took hold of the rope and pulled, wanting the animal to move toward him. The steer continued to back away. Tom couldn't budge it in the right direction.

He let go, disgusted that the animal didn't know he was trying to help. Fear was making it stupid—like a rabbit running into the path of a car instead of away. Then he had an idea. Circling the post in the opposite direction, he reached out to touch the steer's neck. Its skin twitched beneath his fingers.

The steer moved away from him, unwinding the rope a turn. Tom continued nudging it around and around, until the rope was free.

He was pleased with his own cleverness until the steer raised its nose into the air and let loose a bellow so loud and so full of anguish that several cows replied from the corral. Eight seconds later, it bellowed again.

"Ma-a-an!" he muttered. A gooey-looking froth was caught in the corners of its mouth. Maybe it was thirsty.

Tom went into the cooking hut and filled a tin cup from a gasoline can Ignacio's mother used for water. It wasn't much, but maybe it would be enough to keep the steer from bellowing. For a while, at least.

The moonlight seemed to melt into the water,

making it invisible—Tom didn't know it was on the brink of overflowing until it spilled. He crept toward the steer and held out the cup. The animal looked at him sideways, tugging at the rope, backing away. "Come on," Tom encouraged, holding the cup nearer to the animal's snout.

A hand slammed down on his shoulder. Tom grunted and his arm swung around with the rest of him. Water flew from the cup, splashing Ignacio.

"Ai-e-e-e!" Ignacio sputtered. "What are you doing?" Water running down his face and over his mouth made him sound as if he were hissing.

A larger shape appeared behind Ignacio, blotting out the moon. Senor Guerrero held a rifle. The barrel pointed up but a hand cupped the trigger. "*¿Qué pasó?*" he growled.

Tom didn't understand the words, but he understood the question and the anger behind it. "I was . . . I was just getting it . . . the steer . . . some water. To quiet him . . . you know." He waited for Ignacio to explain that to his father. Tom hated the silence that followed. "I . . . I couldn't sleep and . . ."

Ignacio's father interrupted him with a bristling string of Spanish words. When he finished, Ignacio cleared his throat.

"We thought one of the men from La Esperanza

was stealing this animal. Your head . . . you are lucky it doesn't have a hole in it."

Tom began to tremble. It made him shake harder to realize that Ignacio's family considered the threats by the men from La Esperanza real. "I . . . I . . . I'm sorry!"

Ignacio put his hand on Tom's shoulder again, this time gently. "Do you know why this animal is here?"

Tom shook his head.

"This animal must not drink or eat until we kill it. *El estómago*"—he struggled for the English word—"the stomach and *los intestinos* . . . how do you say?"

"Intestines?" Tom guessed.

"*¡Sí! Los* intestines, they must be empty . . . so we can use them . . . to eat."

"*¿Comprendes?*" Senor Guerrero asked, his voice less angry now.

"Do you understand?" Ignacio translated.

Tom nodded, with some queasiness.

"It must be this way," Ignacio continued. He took the cup from Tom's hand. "For us to live in good health, it must die . . . in this way."

"I understand," Tom said, although he wasn't sure that he did.

"*Bueno.*" Ignacio's father grunted and walked

back toward the sleeping hut. Ignacio motioned for Tom to follow.

Livorio had rolled into Tom's place on the mat, so he took Livorio's place beside Ignacio. Soon Ignacio was breathing deeply beside him and Senor Guerrero's snoring rumbled from across the room.

The steer's bellowing was less frequent now, and the sound was weaker. The animal seemed to be giving up and Tom felt the hotness of tears welling in his eyes.

Suddenly, even in this crowded room, Tom had never felt more alone. He felt, deeply, as if the steer were crying out for him, too.

Quietly, he tried to slip from between Livorio and Ignacio. He didn't count on nudging Ignacio with his elbow.

"*¿Qué pasó?*" Ignacio asked, rousing himself, his voice sleepy. "What are you doing?"

"Bathroom . . . I need to go . . . bad," Tom whispered, pleased that such a good excuse had popped into his head. He reached for his shoes.

Ignacio grunted and turned onto his other side. Before Tom could get into a crawling position, Ignacio was softly snoring.

Tom slipped on his shoes, laces dangling, and walked to the steer, which had finally folded its legs and collapsed to the ground. The animal looked over its shoulder halfheartedly and shook its head. Sitting with the steer seemed the right thing to do, the kind thing. He sat with his back leaned up against its back. A shadowy shape seemed to float toward him, close to the ground. It was the dog, who sat next to him, nearer the steer's tail. At the edge of the courtyard, near the cooking hut, Tom saw a sleeping pig. In the moonlight it looked as tight as an unopened sack of cement.

Tom dozed off and on. Before long the steer was calling out only every few minutes—not strongly, its tongue seeming to get in the way. Each time he looked, Tom was surprised that it continued to keep its head up, and neck arched, dignified but dazed.

Several times, Tom was tempted to untie the rope from the post and let the animal go. But he knew, each time, that suffering the anger and disappointment of Ignacio's family would make him feel worse than letting the steer die. It was not a pleasant thing to know about himself. Ignacio and his father had risked danger to save two American kids, not just in the market but now on their own ranch.

And then it occurred to him that unlike the steer, he was not tied to a post in the middle of a courtyard, away from water and food. The steer had been calling to the other cattle—maybe even its own mother. Various cattle had answered from the nearby corral, but the steer couldn't get any closer to them than he was now.

Had he, Tom, been calling to his mother and father in his own silent way? Tom was stunned to think that there was nothing like a rope to stop him from trying to find them. If he could get word to them that he and Philippa were all right and near La Esperanza, his mother and father would be able to figure out how to find them and to keep the men from hurting the Guerreros and destroying their ranch.

Tom didn't know what time it was, but the moon was now so low in the sky that it was half in and half out of the tops of the trees at one end of the courtyard. The pig by the cooking hut was moving more in its sleep. The air seemed to be stirring. It felt to Tom as if the night was ending.

He stood and walked around to face the steer. It seemed not to see him. He bent down on one knee. Its eyes were vacant, like the eyes of people waiting for a movie to start. He gently patted the steer on its soft nose, knowing that he'd never see it again, even if he should return one day to Ignacio's ranch. As he stood, looking down at the steer, he had the same hollow feeling in his stomach as when he saw dogs lying by the side of the road, not knowing if they were alive and suffering, or dead.

Tom looked around the courtyard one last time, turning slowly. When he was facing the road going out, he began walking. He paused only once, to tie his shoes and to make sure he still had money in his pocket.

CHAPTER FIFTEEN

It was several minutes before Tom noticed that the dog was following him. Its tail was up and it looked at him every few seconds, ears cocked forward, as if it expected to be told what kind of adventure they were going on.

Tom was glad of the dog's company. He figured the sounds around them were probably caused only by wind freshening the leaves in the forest. Still, he felt safer with the dog. The farther he got from the Guerreros's ranch, the thicker the undergrowth became, the more it seemed to crowd the road, and the louder the noises grew.

It was hardly a road, anyway. It was more like twin paths, made by two people walking side by side, coming and going, day after day. The dog took one path, and he took the other.

The morning light was getting stronger. Tom imagined that by now Ignacio and his family were getting up. The steer was probably crying out, weaker and drier than before. Tom hoped that nobody would miss him for a while and that Philippa wouldn't be too freaked out when they discovered he was gone. He picked up the pace, wanting to put as much distance between himself and the ranch as possible, not wanting to make it easy for Senor Guerrero to find him and take him back.

Tom tried to remember how far it was to La Esperanza. In spite of the growing light, the road ahead quickly disappeared into gloom, which made it difficult to judge distances. For a moment, he felt as if he were walking the wrong way on a moving sidewalk at the airport, going nowhere.

Swaying ribbons of light dangled from the trees. He almost expected to feel them brush against his face, as if he were walking through the dresses hanging in his mother's closet, as he had when he was little. He passed occasional patches of flower sweetness, reminding him of her perfume.

Should he just walk into La Esperanza—or sneak in? Tom didn't want to be seen by the men who'd visited the ranch. At the same time, he needed to find a place where he could use a telephone. He couldn't remember seeing a police station there. Or a bank or school. Maybe the church, he thought. Surely a priest would help.

He wished he had a hat to hide his blond hair. And was wearing his sunglasses. With them he'd have felt braver.

It was all a muddle—where he would get help and how. But what he was doing was better than doing nothing. Better than waiting around, as the steer was forced to do.

He sighed and turned to say something to the dog. It was gone. Tom hadn't noticed it leaving him. He was disappointed, but more than that it made him nervous. He picked up the pace some, breaking into a sweat, beginning to breathe hard. That made him feel better.

Peering ahead, Tom thought he saw a brightness that he hadn't noticed before. He started to run, pleased to think he was nearing the place where this road connected with the road to the village.

If he hadn't been panting so hard, if his feet hadn't been thumping the ground so loudly, he would have heard the pounding of horse's hooves drawing closer.

"Tom!"

So surprised he almost tripped, Tom slid to a

stop. He turned to see Ignacio pulling back on a rope tied to the horse's face like a halter, bringing the horse from a gallop to a trot. The horse tossed its head, looking much more beautiful in motion than it had standing splay-legged in the corral. But the slower it moved, the more like its old self it looked. Sweat streaking its neck gave the appearance of polished shoe leather, while the rest of its hide looked scuffed and worn.

Ignacio brought the horse alongside Tom and stopped. He leaned forward, resting his elbows on the horse's neck. "What are you doing?" he asked, smiling.

"I'm going to La Esperanza to get some help."

Still smiling, Ignacio shook his head, as if he thought Tom was crazy.

"I don't want your family to get in trouble and I want my parents to know that we're okay."

Ignacio considered this for a moment. "My family, we were all scared. And your sister. We thought maybe the men from La Esperanza took you . . . last night . . . while you were . . ." He smiled. "You should have told us what you are doing."

"But you would have told me I couldn't go."

Ignacio shook his head again, as if this were the craziest thing Tom had said yet. "No," he said. "You are not a prisoner with us. You can come and go when you wish. My father, he might not like what you are doing, but he would not stop you." The horse shuffled away from Tom and Ignacio slapped it on the neck. It settled down. "You are almost a man. My father respects men who are strong . . . here." He thumped his chest.

Tom felt his own chest swell and he smiled in spite of himself. It was a surprise that Senor Guerrero might respect him. Tom pictured him hacking away at undergrowth with his machete, sweat dripping off his face, working so hard for so little. "Is there a telephone there . . . in La Esperanza?"

Ignacio thought for a moment and then nodded. "*Sí,*" he answered, "but it doesn't always work. Come," he said, sitting up and patting the rump of his horse. "My horse is faster than yours."

"But I don't . . ." Tom blurted, before he realized that Ignacio was joking. "Thanks," he said, feeling stupid.

Ignacio reached down and grabbed Tom under his arm. Tom took a little jump and did a belly flop onto the horse. The animal shied as Tom scrambled, swinging his right leg over its rear. The dip in the horse's back slid Tom up against Ignacio.

On its own, the horse began to walk, each step causing Tom to lurch. He grabbed Ignacio around the waist to keep from falling off. Tom felt uncomfortable rubbing up against his friend. He tensed, which made his discomfort worse. Still holding onto Ignacio, he tried to push himself away.

"Relax," Ignacio said, over his shoulder. "Move as the horse moves. Soon, you will be comfortable."

Slowly Tom relaxed. Ignacio was right. The more he relaxed, the more comfortable he felt on the horse, and the less he felt he was crowding Ignacio. Not that Ignacio seemed to mind. Tom had never known anybody who was so comfortable with being close to other people, especially with his brothers and sisters. Tom wished Ignacio was his brother— his and Philippa's.

The road to the village appeared different from horseback than it did from eye level. Being up on the horse, Tom saw more trash along the road, but also more flowers.

Within a few minutes they reached the end of the forest road and turned right onto a road that was wider and looked more heavily traveled. They rode in silence, rocking to the horse's gait. The sun grew hot. Several times, when the road stretched out flat, Ignacio kicked the horse into a trot. Tom's bottom slapped its back. Air exploded from his mouth each time, and Tom grew dizzy, unable to breathe in enough to replace it. The horse began to sweat so much that Tom felt his jeans grow soggy. They clung to him, tugging at his skin where the insides of his legs swung along the horse's sides.

The bell tower of the church was the first sign of La Esperanza. When they came to the outskirts of the village, Tom felt suddenly afraid.

He spoke to the back of Ignacio's head. "What if the men see us? The ones who came to your ranch?"

Ignacio shrugged. "We have a horse. The forest is near."

Ignacio directed the horse down a street. Up ahead, Tom heard children's voices. He leaned to his right and saw a school.

"Look!" Ignacio pointed to a flock of girls jumping rope. They all wore navy skirts and white blouses. Equally surprising, he saw a clump of boys playing tetherball in dark slacks and white shirts, many of them with their hair greased and combed back. Beyond them, several boys had rolled up the legs of their slacks and were kicking a soccer ball back and forth, playing around a dog that was stretched out and sleeping in the middle of the dirt field. Some of the boys looked almost as old as Ignacio.

The school itself was a low cement building with windows made of wooden slats that were lifted open. Bougainvillea shot up like fountains, red flowers spraying over arched doorways that led to classrooms. From some of these rooms came a singsong chorus of voices, sounding like children reciting prayers in church. A few of the girls stared as they went by, but Tom got the impression that he was not a very interesting sight.

"Why aren't you in school?" Tom asked, the school behind them now.

Ignacio shrugged. "I went to school . . . until last year. I can read and write. I study sometimes." Tom remembered the book Ignacio had on his lap at the market and wondered what had happened to it. "I know *la historia Mexicana* . . . you know. Now I must work for my family. In Felicidad and on the ranch. Someday," he added proudly, "the ranch will be mine."

"Oh," was all Tom could say. He knew kids back home who'd dropped out and were working at fast food restaurants or at the mall—if they worked at all. But they were older, sixteen at least. And they seemed sour, unlike Ignacio.

"Do you go to school?" Ignacio asked.

"Yeah," Tom answered.

"Do you work?"

"Um . . . around the house."

"Maybe someday you will have a business?" Ignacio asked.

"Maybe."

Ignacio turned the horse. On their left was a store. Ignacio slid off the horse and tied it to one of the bars guarding the large front window. Not waiting for Tom, he walked toward the store. When Tom slid off, his legs nearly buckled.

Inside, Tom saw an old woman, shorter than he was, handing money to a young man behind a counter. She picked up the looped handles of her string bag and slid them up her arm to the crook of her elbow.

"*Buenos días, Senora Martínez*," Ignacio said.

Frowning, she grunted, her eyes darting from Ignacio to Tom as she walked past them.

Quickly, Ignacio walked up to the counter and spoke to the young man. The young man shrugged and smiled, as if to say, "Sorry."

Ignacio turned to Tom. "You have money. Maybe his telephone will work if we show him money."

Tom dug around in his pocket and pulled up a ball of crumpled bills, hard now from getting wet and drying out so many times. He handed it to

Ignacio. All that was left was the twenty-peso piece. He wanted to keep that.

With a shake of his head, Ignacio placed the money on the counter and once more spoke to the man. The man looked at the bills and then at Ignacio.

"Tell him there will be more money, when my parents come to get me," Tom said. Ignacio nodded and spoke to the young man.

Hesitating for only a moment, the young man's hand went for the money. Before he reached it, his eyes darted from Ignacio to something behind Tom. His hand retreated.

Tom's heart thumped in his chest, seeming to pump all the air from his lungs. He knew who he'd see before he turned around.

Staring at him was the man with the too-small cowboy hat.

CHAPTER SIXTEEN

The man looked at Ignacio and smiled. *"Buenos días, sobrino,"* he said pleasantly.

"Buenos días, tío," Ignacio replied, sounding as if the words were too hot for his mouth.

The man looked at Tom and his smile faded.

Tom's whisper was rough. "How did he know we were here?"

"News travels fast in La Esperanza. I did not think Senora Martínez could walk so fast. Maybe she told a child to run . . . to tell my uncle."

"Your uncle?" Tom stared at the man, trying to see anything resembling Ignacio in his face. His forehead? Yes. And the mouth.

"Sí." Ignacio sighed. "My mother's brother. The ranch belonged to my grandfather before it became ours. He is not a friend of my father."

Tom thought of the threats this man had made to

Senor Guerrero. "He won't really burn down your ranch, will he?"

Ignacio shook his head. "He wants it for himself too much."

Tom was relieved to hear that and was about to say so when the man spoke to Ignacio. His voice was calm, but firm.

Ignacio was not calm. "No!" he interrupted, and then let fly a string of words that looped over his uncle like a lasso. The man's arms stiffened, as if pinned to his sides. Tom wished he knew what Ignacio was saying.

By now, the man looked as angry as Ignacio. His hands were fists, and he looked as if he might use them. The man wasn't much taller than either of them, but much bigger.

"Ignacio," Tom said. "Please. Don't. He'll beat the crap out of you. Look. I'll go with him. There's nothing we can do. And you said he won't hurt your ranch, anyway."

Ignacio shook his head. "This man, this *pig* who calls me his *ne-phew*"—Ignacio spat the last word— "he thinks he is a big man, that he will fight the government. He thinks that he is Pancho Villa and that he will win. But he is only *una mosca* . . . a . . . a *fly*!" He slapped a hand on his forearm, glaring at his uncle, speaking more to him than to Tom. "The soldiers will kill him . . . make him flat . . . like so." He slapped his arm again. "Then they will come to our village and we will never be free of them." He took a step toward his uncle. "*¿Comprende?*" He didn't wait for an answer.

"*¡Basta!*" Senor Cardenas interrupted. Arms still looking as if they were pinned to his sides, he spoke for a few moments. He struggled to remain calm, trying to sound bored, but his face was stiff with anger.

"What is he saying?" Tom asked.

"He is talking about the people suffering and about rich Americans and . . ."

The man stopped and turned his eyes to Tom. They weren't unkind, but they didn't waver. He spoke directly to Tom.

"What is he . . ."

"He is asking you to come . . . alone . . . in peace."

Tom stared at Ignacio's uncle—at his thick neck and his massive arms. What choice did he have? Like the steer, what else could he do? Tom stepped forward.

Ignacio grabbed his arm and pulled him back. "No! I must come with you."

He spoke to the man, who shook his head and then spoke.

"What did he say?"

"He says I cannot come. He says I will make trouble. He wants only you."

Senor Cardenas shrugged off the invisible lasso and stepped toward Tom.

"No!" Ignacio shouted. Ignacio flung himself at the man, head down. He slammed into his uncle's belly.

Senor Cardenas roared and raised his fist to strike. Tom hadn't been in a real fight before—he'd always been afraid of his face getting messed up. But as the man's fist swung down, Tom drew his fist back and let loose with a punch. He'd never hit somebody's face before, and he gasped as pain jolted down his arm.

He was able to swing once more before his own face seemed to explode. Tom's legs gave way and he crumpled to the floor. He sat, dazed, watching Ignacio kick out. Senor Cardenas doubled over.

Tom tried to lift his hands. They were too heavy. Sounds were muffled, and his skin tingled, as if his head were covered by a thick, heavy helmet of shampoo, with a sound like melting suds crackling in his ears. His face began to throb.

With great effort, he stood and staggered toward Ignacio and Senor Cardenas, who was panting and staring at Ignacio, blood trickling from his nose, down his chin.

A hand grabbed Tom from behind. "Hey!" he cried out. Turning, he found himself looking into the face of one of Senor Cardenas's men. Ignacio turned to see what was going on, giving his uncle the opportunity he needed.

Tom heard a thud and saw Ignacio sprawled on the floor, his eyes closed, blood flowing from a split lip. He lurched toward Senor Cardenas, wanting to bellow but croaking instead. The hand on his shoulder tightened its grip and spun him around. He barely had time to close his eyes before his head snapped back. He saw a burst of stars that immediately sank into watery, cold darkness, leaving only ripples of pain behind. It was beautiful, and Tom sighed as he passed out.

Tom woke up in a small room. He was lying on his back and his head throbbed. Sitting up on his elbows, he blinked at light shooting through a window, aimed at him. He wished he had his sunglasses. Only one eye worked. He shifted his weight to touch his other eye and winced. It was swollen shut.

Next to him was Ignacio, lying on his back,

asleep. His shirt was torn and splattered with blood that had sprayed from his nose. The skin around one eye was puffed up and turning from red to purple. Tom wondered if that was how his own eye looked.

The room was stuffy and hot. He looked up to see if there was a fan he could turn on. Hanging from a cord in the ceiling was a lightbulb—nothing more. Tom managed to get himself onto his hands and knees. He scooted to Ignacio, wondering how badly he was hurt. Tom touched him on the shoulder.

"Ignacio!" He pressed harder, beginning to panic. He was relieved when Ignacio snorted and then groaned. Opening a bleary eye, he looked at Tom and tried to smile. Fresh blood bubbled from the crack in his lip.

"Tom!" He struggled to sit up but Tom shook his head, pushing gently against Ignacio's shoulder to keep him down. *"Amigo.* Where are we?"

"I don't know."

Ignacio gazed around with his good eye. "We must get out of here. The window. Can we go out the window?"

With great effort, Tom heaved himself to his feet. A wave of dizziness broke over him and the floor seemed to shift under him like sand. Tom closed his good eye until the sensation passed, then, opening it, he took baby steps to the window. He felt warm air puffing into the room before he could see outside clearly.

Tom turned to Ignacio. "Bars. We can't use the window."

"The door?" Ignacio asked. "Is it locked?"

Tom walked to the door, his steps firmer now, his head a little clearer. He twisted the knob and rattled it. "Locked." He walked to Ignacio and sank to the floor like a balloon letting go of its air.

"I am glad we are together," Ignacio said.

Tom scanned the room, trying to avoid looking at his friend. At least, between the two of them, they had a pair of good eyes. A voice in his head kept saying, There *has* to be a way out. It sounded a lot like Philippa.

"My head!" Ignacio groaned. "Did my uncle play soccer with it?"

Tom wanted to smile, but it hurt too much and he grimaced instead. "Me, too," he said, studying the room.

The walls were cement, painted white, but peeling and stained with mildew. The floor and ceiling were also cement. The window had a metal casing. The room was empty, except for a naked, lumpy mattress pushed into one corner.

Tom's good eye kept returning to the door. It was wood, painted blue. Was it flimsy or sturdy? Would it give way if they threw themselves at it? Did it open in or out? There wasn't a doorjamb inside. Was there one on the outside?

Staring at the door, he tried to decide. The door wasn't square. There were large gaps between the door and the frame around it, all of them uneven. Seeing that, Tom suddenly remembered the one and only time his father had tried to hang a door in their house.

It had been more complicated than any of them had thought it would be. His father had struggled with the door all day. Tom, Philippa, and their mother had checked often on his father's progress. They'd seen very little, but learned some new combinations of bad words. After planing the edges, hoping to make the door fit, Tom's father had finally called on Tom to hold the door so he could screw in the hinges.

Tom's eye was drawn to this door's inside edge. Hinges! Not folded under the door, but fastened so the screws showed on the door and the door frame!

Excited, his breath came in short, fast bursts as he scrambled to his hands and knees.

"*¿Qué pasa?*" Ignacio asked.

Ignoring the question, Tom pulled himself onto his feet at the door. The screw heads were big and the groove in the top was wide.

He looked down at his jeans. Would the button work as a screwdriver? How about the rivet at the top of a pocket?

And then he thought of the twenty-peso coin.

"What are you doing?" Ignacio asked. He sounded worried.

"I think we can get out of here!" Tom panted. His head was pounding and he wished he could sit down. Instead he reached into his pocket and pulled out the coin. "If we can unscrew the hinges, I think we can take off the door!"

Ignacio grunted. "*¡Qué bueno!*" He looked at Tom with both surprise and respect. "This is perfect!" He scooted closer to Tom, who was trying to make the coin fit into the slot of a screw.

Tom groaned. "It's too thick." He was about to throw the coin onto the floor in disgust when an idea struck him. Holding the coin firmly in both hands, he began scraping its edge against a bare patch on the cement wall.

The coin was hard. Soon his fingers ached and his arms began to slow. He paused and was glad to see that the edge was sharper, narrower.

He slipped the coin into a slot and began to twist. The coin popped out twice before he was able to press it far enough in to try turning. A drop of sweat fell into his eye, stinging, but he blinked it away and kept increasing the pressure on the coin. Just as his fingers began to tremble, the screw gave.

"I got it!" he shouted.

"Quiet!" Ignacio ordered. "They will hear us and come see what is happening."

Tom nodded. Working quickly now, he watched the screw rise from the hinge until it clattered to the floor. "One down and"—he quickly counted— "eight to go."

They took turns, and with each screw, Tom felt his strength returning. Ignacio was able to loosen the screws faster than he could, so they soon fell into a pattern: Ignacio attacking each screw and Tom extracting it. The first two screws tore up the coin so much that Tom had to sharpen another part of its edge.

They saved the top hinge for last because it would be the hardest to reach.

"Climb onto my back," Tom suggested. "That way you can really lean into the screw."

Ignacio nodded just as they heard a key slipping into the lock outside, and, with a click, turn.

Tom and Ignacio leaped toward the mattress and flopped down, almost knocking heads. Tom watched the door. "Run outside if it falls off," he whispered. Ignacio nodded.

Teetering slightly on its hinge, the door opened slowly, just enough for a cloth-covered plate to slide in. The door closed just as slowly, and the lock shot into its hole with a clunk.

Grinning at each other, Ignacio's lip so scabbed now that it didn't bleed, they each grabbed a still-warm tortilla from under the cloth on their way back to the door. Tottering on Tom's back, Ignacio loosened the last three screws and stepped off, handing Tom the coin. He got down on his hands and knees, ready for Tom to climb onto his back, but Tom shook his head. "I think I can get it from here."

In less than a minute, the door's bottom edge hit the floor with a gentle thud. Tom slipped the coin back into his pocket.

Holding their breath, both pressing an ear against the still-upright wood, they listened for sounds outside. Not hearing anything, they wiggled out the hinged edge of the door until the bolt slipped from its keeper. Peering through the strip of light that flooded through the door frame, they checked to see if anybody was outside before sliding the door aside and stepping outside.

Tom had never smelled air so fresh or seen light so beautiful. But the pleasure of these things was replaced by panic. "I think we should put it back, you know, so they won't notice," he whispered.

Ignacio shook his head, looking around. "We don't have time. We must run. This way."

Pain shooting through their bodies, they hurried around the back of the little house where they'd been locked up. A startled chicken shrieked and flew away from them. A naked boy looked up from playing with rocks in the dirt street. A few steps later, Ignacio dropped into a gully that ran behind a house surrounded by the yeasty, sweet smell of baking bread. This gully led to a larger one, where they turned left. Tom struggled to keep up, hurting with every step, trying to keep his one good eye focused.

"Up there," Ignacio croaked, pointing, "we will climb out, onto the road. We must be careful going back to my family's ranch. We must listen for cars and hide in the forest."

Tom and Ignacio hurried along the edge of the road, keeping in shadows, once scrambling into the forest when they heard a rumbling. It was only an airplane flying overhead.

The way back seemed twice as long. Tom and Ignacio didn't talk, saving all their energy for trotting, walking, limping, trotting, walking, limping. Tom sucked at his own saliva, swallowing it to satisfy his growing thirst. Too soon, even the spit in his mouth dried up. When dusk began to fall, Tom felt his energy fading, disappearing with the light. How much farther did they have to go? At that moment, the arched gate to the Guerreros's ranch magically appeared up ahead. His legs began to run, as if on their own, as if they belonged to somebody else.

Ignacio beat Tom to the courtyard, yelling, "*¡Mamá! ¡Papá!*"

Tom staggered beside his friend and saw Edgardo standing beside the shadowy lump that was the steer. Its head barely hovered above the ground. Philippa and the other children sat side by side, leaning against its back.

Spotting him, Philippa shrieked with pleasure. She jumped to her feet and ran up to him, almost knocking him over. She gave him a fierce hug and then shoved away from him. Her face was suddenly pinched with anger.

"Why did you leave? How could you!" She stomped her foot. "I *hate* you!" she yelled, throwing herself on him again, and hugging him even tighter. Her arms loosened and she looked up, the anger gone, replaced by squinting surprise. "What happened to your face?"

Senor Guerrero walked up to them before Tom had time to answer. The man studied them for a moment. His face broke into a smile, making him almost as unrecognizable as one of the masks he sold in Felicidad. He spoke a few words to Ignacio.

"My father says that he will take you and Philippa to Felicidad." Philippa squealed with delight. Ignacio waved his hand to quiet her. "But later," he said. "First he must offer to drink some mescal with my uncle in La Esperanza, to talk of boys who run off and disgrace their fathers." Ignacio smiled. "My father, he says he will pay for the drinks and that my uncle will be talking in his sleep before long." Ignacio turned to ask his father a question. Grinning, he looked at Tom with his one good eye. "He says I can come."

CHAPTER SEVENTEEN

Wednesday. On a Mexican beach. Puffs of warm air gently lift the bleached hair sticking through the rash scabs on his forearm. A startling blue sky. Sunlight crisping his new shirt.

Yet miserable.

Tom pushed his new sunglasses to the top of his nose. His eye was still swollen, but at least the skin didn't push up against the lens on the inside anymore. Sometimes he even forgot how bad his face looked until he saw people's puzzled faces.

He tumbled the twenty-peso coin from one hand to the other. Its mangled edges were sharp against his skin. He'd meant to give it to Ignacio when he'd said good-bye to him several hours ago—more for a joke than anything else. Or something to remember him by. It was, after all, only small change, hardly worth anything.

Ignacio and his father were probably back at the

ranch by now. They were going to slaughter the steer today. Maybe the steer was already dead. Tom was glad that his last view of the steer had been of its legs folded under it, its head held with great dignity.

"Hey, Tom!"

Tom looked up to see Philippa running toward him, her new white smock glowing. It had flowers embroidered around the neck, not animals, but otherwise it was the same as the one she'd lost in the market.

"Hey, Tom! The taxi's here!"

Tom nodded. "I'll be right there," he said. "Tell Mom and Dad that I'll be right there."

"Okay," Philippa said. "But if you don't come soon, we'll leave without you."

"Be sure to visit me the next time you and Mom and Dad come back here," Tom said.

Philippa grinned. "Can I stay, too?"

Tom chuckled. "Look, Filly. Go tell Mom and Dad I'll be there in a few minutes. I just need a few more minutes. Okay?"

Philippa nodded and ran toward the hotel—up the beach, over the spot where she and Gordon had made the castle. Tom dug at the sand with his feet, letting it sift between the leather strips of his huaraches. It was tempting—being left behind. He could walk up the beach and become one of the fly specks he saw now. Tomorrow he could walk to town, to the market, to the Guerreros's stall where Ignacio and his father might be bargaining with an American tourist wanting to buy the mask of an angel that looked as if it were about to puke.

But he knew that in less than eight hours, including a stopover in St. Louis, he'd be home.

Where it was cold and there was snow on the ground.

Home.

Back in his room. Getting ready to sleep in his own bed.

Home.

Somehow, home didn't seem as real as the Guerrero ranch. As real as Ignacio and his family—the children playing, *Mamá* making tortillas, *Papá* hacking away at undergrowth with his machete. As real as the steer crying out, thirsty and alone. As real as fighting Senor Cardenas and getting his face bashed in. As real as the scary ride from La Esperanza to Felicidad, only one headlight working, shining more up and out than down on the road, Senor Guerrero smelling of mescal and pleased with himself.

He wondered if he would feel as close to his family there, back in Minnesota, as he had here for the last couple of days.

He sensed someone approaching. He looked up. The boy stopped. He was still wearing a Cowboys T-shirt and tiny gym shorts with frayed purple piping around the edges. His hair was still stringy with dirt.

The boy smiled and held out a carved stone elephant. "Four *dólares, amigo,*" he said, in his soft lisp.

Tom nodded. Putting the coin in his left hand, he reached into the pocket of his jeans with his other. He pulled out a ten-dollar bill his father had given him for the trip back home.

The boy's eyes grew large.

Tom held it out.

The boy pulled out some money and began to count change.

Tom shook his head. "No. Here. Take it. Please."

The boy took the money, looking puzzled. His face suddenly brightened and he took two more carvings from the cloth bag he carried. He looked at Tom hopefully.

Tom shook his head. "No. Just that." He pointed to the elephant and held out his other, empty, hand.

But the boy shook his head even harder and plunked all three figures in his palm.

"No. No. You don't understand . . ."

"*Gracias,*" the boy interrupted, bowing. As he walked away, he began whistling.

"Tom!" It was his father this time. Tom glanced at his watch. It was getting late.

"Coming!" he called back, glancing at the twenty-peso coin in his left hand. Like him, it looked as if it had been in a fight. He smiled and slipped it into his pocket.

He turned to wave at his father, who was waving to him from the hotel's terrace. There were black smudges on the white paint from the fire that had burned part of the hotel. Several coconut trees nearby looked like spent matches stuck into the sand, their knobby ends drooping.

He glanced around one last time. From the corner of his good eye he saw a soldier approach, walk-marching up the beach, a cocky smile on his face. Strutting seagulls scattered as he drew near, mewing like peeved cats as they flew into the air. The soldier looked at him and Tom stared back. The soldier wasn't much older than he was. When he nodded, Tom refused to nod back, turning instead to look at the sea. Shards of light shot from the water. Waves thumped. Tom swallowed a lump in his throat.

Then, holding the carved figures in one hand, he

started for the hotel. The turtle for Henderson. The dolphin for Laura. The elephant for himself. He'd take the Made in China stickers off the turtle and dolphin, but leave it on the elephant.

Stepping over a dead fish tangled in a clump of seaweed, he broke into a stiff run.